CYBER WRITERS

AND THE ZEBRA OF LIFE

D1010308

KAREN KOSTLIVY

3L Publishing
Sacramento, California

Library of Congress Control Number: 2010924014

ISBN-13: 978-0-615-36226-7

Cyber Writers soft-cover edition 2010

Printed in the United States of America

For more information about special discounts for bulk purchases, please contact 3L Publishing at 916.300.8012 or log onto our website at www.3LPublishing.com.

Cover illustration by Cynthia McKeith and Tom McKeith

Book design by Erin Pace

To my two suns, Camron and Masson — you're the lights of my life … and to my mother Marilyn Kostlivy.

Acknowledgments

To bring "Cyber Writers" to fruition it has been an adventure in itself. Stolen laptops, computer crashes and lost data; well, that is another story, however, true. It has taken a team of wonderful people to bring you Cyber Writers.

First, I would like to thank God for bringing into my life the awesome cast of characters that collaborated with me on this fantastic journey.

I am extremely grateful to the fabulous ladies behind 3L Publishing, Michele Smith (1L) and Michelle Gamble Risley (2L), and their wonderful team; Malia Grigsby, project manager and Erin Pace, graphic designer. Michelle (2L) you are a fabulous editor (I promise no more whiny boys).

Thank you to my illustrators, Cynthia McKeith and Tom McKeith — you did an outstanding job with the illustration on the cover.

My sincerest thanks to Brooklynn Nabeta, my ghost writer for this book; she truly has a wonderful gift and is an amazing wordsmith.

Special thanks to Eric, Stephany and Jennifer Jordan and Janice White, for their tremendous support, advice and friendship. You're truly great friends.

Of course, I need to thank my husband Davis, for editing all the drafts and his continual support of all my adventures. And my thanks to Tim May for his keen eye. I would also like to thank my two nieces, Mikala Kostlivy, Bailey Ramsey, my nephew Nolan Otis, and my two sons Camron and Masson for all of their feedback and for reading the story over and over again.

I would like to thank my little sister Lisa Cole for her help and introducing me to Mrs. Kathleen Stewart. Kathleen took zillions of phone calls, e-mails and unannounced visits from me. She inspired me to continue the journey. Kathleen, I am so ever grateful to you for seeing what I didn't see, thank you.

Karen Kostlivy
March 2010

Pronunciation Index

Akili

Pronunciation: (ah KEE lee)

Meaning: Wisdom, intellect, sense

Jelani

Pronunciation: (jeh LAH nee)

Meaning: Great, mighty, powerful

Lutalo

Pronunciation: (LOO tah loh)

Meaning: Fighter, warrior

Mwamba

Pronunciation: (m WAM bah)

Meaning: Strong, powerful

Sebahive

Pronunciation: (seh ba HEE vay)

Meaning: Bearer of good fortune

1

MASON WITT SAT AT THE BACK OF A HOT, MUSTY SCHOOL BUS. His seat was sticky and smelled of tuna sandwiches and old milk. Paper airplanes, pencil erasers, leftover lunch bits, and various small toys whizzed through the air in all directions. His daily bus rides had caused him to become quite good at dodging stray, flying objects. The regular bouncing, screaming and singing from the other kids always reminded Mason of the monkeys he had seen on a field trip to the zoo. Out of the window he saw the bright green Queens Avenue street sign. "Almost there," he said to himself. He couldn't wait to get home. It was finally the day he could get back on his skateboard.

Mason's mother had grounded him for a week for skateboarding in their neighbor's empty swimming pool without her permission. Being deprived from his board the entire time had driven him practically crazy. He loved the way the wind smacked against his face whenever he and his best friend Cole practiced together in old Mr. and Mrs. Johnson's pool. He closed his eyes and remembered gliding between the deep and shallow ends, high-fiving Cole as they crossed each other in the middle — and even suffering a few magnificent wipeouts.

"Hey, are you asleep?" Mason heard someone say. He opened his eyes and turned to his left. A bigger boy with giant, black glasses was staring him in the face.

"Oh, hey, Adam. No, I wasn't sleeping, just dreaming," said Mason.

"I like day dreaming," piped Adam.

"What are you drawing?" Mason asked.

"A collage of animals," Adam replied.

"Let me take a look," Mason reached out his hand taking the sketch pad from Adam.

"Awesome!" Mason voiced. "Unbelievable, I can't believe this. I can see a zebra and then I can't. You can really draw dude." said Mason as he handed the pad back to Adam.

Adam had started to stand up when the bus suddenly came to a hard, jerky stop. He and Mason were both launched forward in their seat from the sharpness of it. Sitting up straight, Mason saw another bright green street sign outside of his window. It was the one he had been waiting for.

"See you!" He shouted as he rushed down the aisle. He

jumped out of the bus, skipping the three steps, and walked hurriedly up Stabler Lane.

Two-story buildings, that looked to Mason like doll houses, lined both sides of the street. They all looked the same except for the paint color. Each had a small front lawn, and tall trees that made them almost invisible from the sidewalk. Mason ran up the front walkway of number 708. It was the only olive green house on Stabler Lane. Opening the front door, he shouted, "Mom, I'm home."

Mason dropped his backpack in the front foyer and walked into the kitchen. His mother was looking in the refrigerator for apples and peanut butter — Mason's favorite after-school snack.

"Hey, Boo. How was your day?" she asked without looking up.

"Boring. And jeez Mom. Don't call me that all right. What's up with Dad? Is he home?"

"Are you missing him?"

"Yeah … this trip's too long."

"It will be great when he comes home. No worries, it's not much longer."

"Yeah, OK."

"Do you have any homework?"

"Nope. Did it on the bus."

"Good we have errands to run." She stood up straight and

closed the refrigerator to give Mason a hug. "Mason, your hair. Come on. Don't you care about how you look? Seriously comb your hair."

Mason's mother had tried daily to get him to neatly fix his hair. "Why don't you try parting it on the side? Or maybe put some gel in it," she would say. But Mason always shrugged away the suggestions. He liked the way his hair looked when he didn't comb it. He liked to keep clean, but he liked his clothes and hair to look messy. He teased his mother by running his fingers through his thick, wavy, blond hair, trying to mess it up even more.

"Oh, stop that," she pleaded. "Well, at least you're getting a haircut today."

"What time?"

"We need to leave here in about an hour. We have to pick up your brother from karate and go to the grocery store, too."

"Can I skate until then?"

"Absolutely not. You're still grounded."

"No I'm not. Yesterday was my last day."

His mother thinks for a moment. "I suppose."

"I'm gonna get my board right now!"

"Okay, but hurry. Remember we have to leave soon. Take your food and put your backpack in your room before you go outside."

Mason grabbed the plate of sliced apples and peanut

butter. His mom had arranged the apple slices in a circle around the plate with the peanut butter in the center just as Mason loved it: his big fruit flower. He looked at his plate — a neat circle of sliced apples with peanut butter in the center — and wonders when his mother will stop treating him like a baby. He has learned to quit pointing it out. She will keep doing it — and he feels kind of guilty when she looks all sad and discouraged, but really it's kind of embarrassing he thinks as he heads upstairs. Walking upstairs to his room, Mason stuffed an entire slice covered with peanut butter into his mouth. His cheeks were so full he could hardly chew. With his backpack on his right arm and his apples on the plate in his left hand, Mason stumbled into his bedroom. He tossed the backpack onto his bed and set the plate down on his desk and turned on his laptop computer. Since his bus ride had left him smelling like rotten milk and sandwiches, he decided to change clothes before doing anything else.

Mason noticed the screen of his laptop flashed a new message. The new message in his inbox was from Cyber Writers-Africa and was marked URGENT! He had been a member of an international cyber pen pal club for as long as he could remember and had received e-mails and text messages from all over the world, but never one from Africa. Mason was so overwhelmed with excitement that he almost choked on the apple slice still in his mouth. He grabbed his laptop, leaped onto his bed and started to click on the icon to the inbox to open his new message, being careful not to hit the delete button by mistake. Just as his finger was ready to click on the key to open his new message his mother burst into his room.

"Mason, we've got to go now! I made a mistake. Your haircut is in 20 minutes, and we still have to get your brother first!"

"But, Mom, I …"

"Come on let's go."

Wanting to savor the new message for later, Mason decided to leave his laptop at home. He quickly changed his shirt and rushed downstairs.

On the way to the karate studio, he tried to remember everything he had learned about Africa. "I know there are pyramids. The Nile River is longest river in the world. What else?" He thought. Before he knew it, his mother had pulled into the studio's parking lot.

"Will you please go in and get Jamie?" Asked his mother. "He doesn't know we're picking him up early. And hurry, please!"

Mason jumped out of the car and ran up to the front door of the dojo. As he entered the building, he could hear numerous voices all shouting "Hiyah!" in unison. He tiptoed down a hallway and peeked into the second room on the right. His brother was in the very front of the class demonstrating a roundhouse kick. Mason crept into the room, waved to Jamie, and mouthed the words "Let's go." Jamie nodded to Mason, bowed to his teacher, and bounced over to his duffle bag over an invisible hop-scotch pattern.

"What's going on?" he asked.

"We both have to get a haircut *right now.*"

Jamie slung his bag over his shoulder. It was almost bigger than him. "Let's go!" He said, as he skipped out the door and all the way to the car.

Mason began to tense up as they drove to the barber shop. Knowing he would have to wait for hours until he could read his new message was driving him crazy. He felt a little better, though; when he saw that Ben the Barber would be cutting his hair that day. Mason had always liked Ben. He seemed to know so much about all things and always had an answer to either of the Witt brothers' questions. Mason once asked him why he was a barber when he could probably do anything in the world. Ben had smiled and answered, "I just really like cutting hair."

"Do you know anything about Africa?" Mason asked as Ben began cutting his hair.

"Sure. It's a beautiful continent. One of my seven favorites," he answered with a wink. "Why do you ask?"

Mason explained all about his urgent e-mail, and how he

could not wait to get home and read it.

"So, you've got a new one. And from Africa too!" said Ben.

"I can hardly wait, and we still have to go to the grocery store!" Mason complained.

"Patience young man," Ben said as he snipped hair and smiled. "You're a wild one all right." He lifted hair, cut and shook his head.

Mason felt kind of proud of the fact and grinned but didn't answer.

"All finished," Ben said as he dusted bits of hair off Mason's shoulders. "You be sure to tell me all about Africa."

"Sure," said Mason sliding off the chair.

Before they left, Ben gave Mason and Jamie a homemade caramel for a treat. Jamie had gotten a trim at the same time from Leticia. He liked her a little bit better than Ben because she was a lot more talkative, and he liked how her hair was always a different color every time he saw her, sometimes pink, green or orange. She was always interested to hear about his karate lessons too. Walking out the door with their mother, Mason and Jamie thanked Ben and Leticia.

"See you later, Leticia. Next time make your hair purple!" Said Jamie.

"We'll see," laughed Leticia.

"Race you to the car, Jamie," said Mason, trying to hurry

things up. "1, 2, 3 … GO!"

Mason ran a little slower than he could. He liked to let Jamie win at some things.

"I win! I win!" Cried Jamie.

"Yeah, well … first is the worst and second is the best," Mason teased.

At the grocery store, everything reminded Mason of his e-mail and Africa. He saw a giant display of toilet paper that reminded him of the pyramids, and the red and yellow bag of animal crackers Jamie had grabbed reminded him of the African wildlife. He was so excited and wanted to go home, which made him hyper and fidgety. His mother looked at him with annoyance — he was close to getting on her nerves. When it was time to check out, Mason helped bag all of the groceries and tried convincing Jamie to help.

"Help me!" Mason ordered.

"Why? It's not my job."

"Oh!" Groaned Mason. "I just want to go home."

"Who cares," replied Jamie in hopes of goading his big brother just a little more.

"I got an urgent e-mail … from Africa," as Mason said it his mind wandered to the world of giraffes, lions and tigers. Jamie, completely disinterested, found the animal crackers and opened them. Just as he was about to stuff one in his mouth, his mother protested.

"Jamie, no," warned his mother. "After dinner."

"What is for dinner?" He asked.

"Pizza."

"Yeah!" Cried Jamie.

"No!" Moaned Mason.

"What's wrong with you? You love pizza," said his mother.

"I know, but I want to get home and read my e-mail. Can't we get it to go?"

"All right. What's in the e-mail?" She frowned at him, wondering what was more important than pizza and flashing on thoughts of predators.

"Nothing."

"Not nothing …" She waited.

"Oh! Fine," he relented. "I got an urgent e-mail from a new Cyber Writer from Africa …" His voice trailed off as he pondered those elephants.

"Africa?" Mother questioned. "It's not some scam artist asking for money, is it!? You know not to answer those e-mail requests, right?"

Mason groaned, "Yes, can we go home now?"

"But it will cost you."

"Fine. How much?"

"Three."

"Three! Okay, but I don't want any change back."

Mason then gave his mom three kisses on the cheek. It was

their family tradition to pay for small favors with hugs and kisses. Mason felt like he was too old for it; but he was willing to do anything to get home faster. It took a half an hour to get the pizza and get home — to Mason it felt like forever.

"Can I please eat in my room?" He asked.

"Sure," said his mom. Mason grabbed two slices and a napkin and sprinted up to his room. He slammed the door shut, set down his pizza, and picked up his laptop.

"Finally," he whispered.

2

MASON CAREFULLY CLICKED ON THE CURSER TO OPEN HIS NEW MESSAGE and waited for it to appear on the screen. As he waited he thought he saw bits of dust and dirt fall onto his bed.

"Wow, they even sent me a bit of the place," Mason smirked aloud. He lay on his bed and at last began to read.

Dear Mason Witt,

Greetings and jambo to you. Jambo is how you say hello where I am from. My name is Lutalo* and I am 14 years old. I live in a large village in Africa. I wish to tell you that my village is beautiful, and that everyone lives together in peace, but now I cannot. Not very long ago it was, but now that our Zebra of Life has been stolen, our land and people have been suffering. You see, the Zebra is what brings prosperity to our farmers' crops and harmony to all of the villagers. It *is because of the Zebra that our village thrives. But three weeks ago, some strange men came to our village. They told us they had heard of our Zebra of Life and only wished to see it for themselves. They were very kind and pretended to be our friends. We even invited them into our homes and fed them. But on their first night with us, they stole the Zebra while everyone was sleeping. Now our village is failing. Our crops are dying, and everyone fights now. The Zebra's absence has made everyone angry, and now they have trouble getting along with each other. Everyone is especially angry with my father, Mwamba*, because he is the one who invited the strangers to stay in our village. Ever since the Zebra was stolen, our three strongest and bravest men, including my father, have gone in search of it. The other men have returned, but my father has not. I am scared that he might be dead.*

Mason couldn't believe what he was reading. He knew what it felt like to have your Dad away and to miss him. "Man I wish I could help Lutalo," he thought tinkering with ideas that were very likely impossible since he didn't have the money to fly there — and he didn't think Mom would send him either.

"Hey! You have school tomorrow," said his mother as she stopped and peered into the room. "Don't forget to brush your teeth."

"Can I finish reading my e-mail first?"

"Finish and bed."

"Yeah, okay."

"Night."

"Goodnight, Mom."

With her head still in Mason's doorway, she shouted for Jamie to come and say goodnight.

"Coming!" Jamie yelled. Mason could hear Jamie's footsteps coming quickly toward his bedroom. He burst through the door with a set of toy bow and arrows and jumped headfirst onto Mason's bed, almost knocking the laptop out of his hands.

"Hey!" Shouted Mason. "Be careful!"

Jamie stood up and started jumping on the bed. "What ya doin'?" He asked.

"I was trying to read my e-mail!"

"Can I read it?"

"I haven't finished it yet."

"Well, what's it say so far?"

"Stop jumping and maybe I'll tell you."

Jamie plopped down onto the bed. "Okay, I'm ready," he said.

Jamie's eyes grew wider and wider as he listened to Mason explain all about Lutalo and the Zebra of Life, and how Lutalo's father had not returned from his search for it.

"That's really cool," he said. He reached behind him and handed Mason the plastic bow and arrows. "Here, send these. You can take it and …" he fell backwards, holding his throat like he couldn't breathe, acting out some melodramatic death scene, and falling to the ground with his tongue hanging out. "Kill 'em. Shoot 'em up! Bang! Bang! Just like you do lions."

"Jamie, you can't run around killing people!" Mason objected and rolled his eyes.

Jamie squinted his eyes and smiled. "Just kidding. But still send those to him, okay?"

"Sure," said Mason, trying to appease his little brother. "Go to bed, and I'll tell you the rest in the morning."

"Yeah! Okay, `night." Jamie hopped off the bed and hurled himself across the room, shutting the door on the way out.

Mason yawned and settled back into his bed. He turned off the lamp on his nightstand, pulled the covers over his head and his laptop, and started to read.

I pray every night that my father will return with the Zebra of Life, and that our village will be restored, but I get worried as each day passes and he does not come home. Before my father left, he told me where he was going to look for the men and the Zebra. I know the way there, and I want to go and look for him, but I can't do it alone, and no one else in the village is willing to go with me.

Mason stopped reading. "Teeth," he said with a groan. He threw the blankets off of his head and jumped out of bed, landing on something cold and spongy.

"Ugh! What is that?" He cried. He took his flashlight and shined it onto his feet. Green moss and rocks surrounded him. He waved his flashlight around frantically. The walls of his room were beginning to melt away like candle wax. Screeches of monkeys, laughter of hyenas, chirping of insects, and trumpeting of elephants resounded in his ears.

"What the …?" He shouted and jumped back onto his bed, landing on Jamie's bow and arrows. He shut his eyes as tight as he could. "Wake up, wake up," he frantically whispered; but the sounds persisted. He could feel his bed starting to dissolve away from under him. Clutching the toys and his flashlight, he rolled onto the ground. Slowly opening his eyes, he could see that he was no longer in his bedroom at all. He was griped in fear and thought if he could just stay still, not make a move, he might wake up, and it would be all gone. Just some weird freaky dream … you know because he just read that message from Lutalo.

He opened his eyes. He looked around some more. Still there, he thought. Everything had changed. His bedroom walls, his desk, dresser, skateboard and laptop were all gone. Even the bow and arrows in his hand had changed. Instead of Jamie's plastic toys, Mason held gleaming golden arrows and a shimmering ivory bow. Mason had never seen more beautiful weapons in his life — not even in a museum. "Wow," he whispered, as he ran his fingers over his weaponry. He staggered to his feet and began to walk, looking for people.

He reached out and touched the jungle brush. Felt real. He then tentatively looked up at the canopy of overgrown foliage that shielded the jungle floor from direct sunlight. He looked around and wasn't sure what to do. Should he stay or go? A distant "screech" startled him, and a big, brown hairy bug flew right in front of him. He waved his arm to protectively drive it off. He was disoriented and stepped forward, "crunch," as he tried to make his way through the thick overgrowth. He touched a smooth tree trunk that was buttressed for support in the absence of deep roots. He curiously pulled down a broadleaf that was big, flat and thin. He looked around some more — everything was big and overgrown and damp, with vines dangling everywhere and in his way to climb through. His curiosity moved him to explore his surroundings.

At last, he came to the edge of the jungle. Barren, dead land stretched out wide in front of him. Far ahead, in the middle of the lifeless environment, he could see what looked like a large village. "What is this place? How did I get here?" he thought. He suddenly saw a small figure racing toward him and shouting.

"He's here! He's here!" Cried the figure.

"What? Who's here? Is he talking to me?" Mason felt confused as he thought. The small figure ran straight up to Mason and abruptly stopped. It was an African boy, about eight years old, with soft brown eyes and a big, bright smile.

"You're here!" He said, giving Mason a smile that stretched across his entire face.

"Here?" Mason asked.

"Africa!" The boy cried in elation. "You came to save us. You will help us find the Zebra of Life."

"Whoa! What! What are you talking about?"

"The Zebra of Life!" The boy cried and started pulling him. Mason resisted.

"Where are you going?"

"Taking you to Lutalo!"

"The guy in the e-mail?"

"Yes, come …"

The boy continued to tug Mason forward toward the village. Mason resisted. "I don't want to go."

"You must! Come!" The boy would not be dissuaded.

Mason reluctantly relented and allowed the boy to pull him by the arm. Yellow-and-brown fields of rotting crops lined their way. Everything had putrefied and wilted into decay. Hundreds of flies swarmed over the moldering harvest, several flew at Mason's face as if they were trying to attack him.

"It stinks!" Protested Mason, holding his nose.

The small boy lowered his head. "I know, but we can't do anything to help the crops. We have tried many things, but without the Zebra of Life nothing in our village can survive, not even friendships."

As they entered the town, Mason saw numerous groups of people standing in the streets, shouting, waving their arms around, and spitting at each other's feet. Mason shuddered at all of the fighting that encircled him and the boy.

"I see Lutalo!" Cried the boy, as he pulled Mason over to a small, rickety hut. "Lutalo, Lutalo, look who it is! I found him!"

Another African boy who looked closer to Mason's own age was sitting in front of the hut in a large chair made of dead, twisty tree branches woven together. The chair reminded Mason of a king's throne; but one that had been broken quite a few times and fixed with heaps of mud. The boy stood from his chair and smiled. "Jambo! Mason," he greeted Mason with a wide smile.

Mason stood there frozen not sure what to say or do. Lutalo grabbed his hand and shook it with fierce enthusiasm. "This is American, yes?"

"What?"

"Handshake?"

"Oh, oh yeah." Mason looked down with a shrug and felt his tension start to release.

"I'm Lutalo! So happy to meet you," he said in a stilted way as if he had heard this version of English from some old tape on language. "Thank you, Sebahive*," said Lutalo, nodding to the small boy who was still holding onto Mason's elbow. "He's my little bearer of good news."

Sebahive lifted his chin and smiled, then dashed away as quickly as he had first appeared to Mason.

"I just knew you would come," said Lutalo, looking back to Mason. "I didn't expect it to be this soon, but that is even better!"

"How did I get here? What is this place?"

Lutalo looked puzzled by such a question. "What do you mean? You know how you got here."

"Umm, no, no I don't. I'm in my room one minute and then here."

Lutalo laughed with an infectious nature. He didn't seem puzzled and nodded. "Ah, but you are here, right? You will help us, yes?"

"Help? With what?"

"The Zebra of Life, of course." Lutalo's smile never left his face.

Mason was downright puzzled now. He wasn't sure what he should do or say or how he got here; but Lutalo seemed pleasantly pacified and accepted Mason's presence as a simple given. Mason stared at him and Lutalo stared back —

same jovial smile of acceptance. Mason's patience ran thin. "Okay, okay, so what do I do?"

Lutalo nodded. "Good. We knew you would."

"So okay … now what?" Mason was confused.

"You help! Find the Zebra and then my father, right!" Lutalo looked at the bow and arrow. "Your bow and arrows should help."

"Oh my brother Jamie gave me these."

"Here, you can carry them in this." Lutalo handed Mason a large, dark red, leather shoulder bag that had been hanging from his throne of branches.

"Cool!" said Mason.

"It's the least I can do for you now. I can't tell you how grateful I am," said Lutalo. "Let's get …" Lutalo was suddenly cut off by a loud shrieking sound.

"What was that?!" Mason yelled.

"It came from back there. Where you came from," said Lutalo.

"You mean from that jungle?"

"Yes! Come on! Let's see what it is."

As Mason raced after Lutalo, he felt adrenalin coursing through his veins. He strangely wasn't afraid anymore. In fact, he felt himself smiling as he chased after Lutalo. He was an adrenalin junkie anyway — this should be fun, it suddenly occurred to him — the beginning of a great adventure. His courage up — he was ready for it. The two boys ran as fast as they could out of the village and into the edge of the jungle.

3

MASON RACED BEHIND LUTALO INTO A LABYRINTH OF GREEN, JUNGLE FOLIAGE. He wanted to tell Lutalo to slow down, but he could hardly speak. He had never seen another kid his age run so fast. As they darted deeper and deeper into the jungle, the shrieking sound began to fade away. Suddenly, Lutalo stopped running. He held up his hand for Mason to stop behind him.

"What's wrong?" Mason asked, almost completely out of breath.

"It's just that I can't hear that sound anymore. It's gone," said Lutalo without even looking back at Mason. Mason bent over, placing his hands on his knees, panting and sweating. "Are you all right?" asked Lutalo.

"Yeah ... I'll be ... fine. I just ... need a second," Mason huffed. "I don't think ... I've ever run that fast ... in my life!"

"Should I slow down for you?"

"No! No. I'm okay," said Mason, straightening up but wincing slightly from a cramp. "Hey, by the way, where exactly in Africa are we?"

"Right now we are on the border of the Congo Jungle."

"Do you know your way through this jungle? I mean how are we going to be able to find the Zebra of Life and your dad?"

Lutalo smiled. "Don't worry. Come on. Let's keep moving."

The two ventured further, past miles and miles of gigantic trees and vines that reached so high that Mason could not even see where they stopped — above or ahead. To Mason, everything was big, even bigger than he could have imagined. The leaves, shrubs, flowers and especially the bugs were all bigger than his whole head. He was also amazed at how quickly Lutalo navigated the tangle of giant jungle plant life.

"Are you sure this is the right way?" He asked.

Lutalo stopped walking. "No. Well, I mean … I think it is right, but I am not sure."

"What!? You mean we're going the wrong way?" Mason protested.

"I think we'll … wait a minute. Yes, that's it! I had almost forgotten!" Said Lutalo, as his eyes brightened with excitement.

"Forgotten what?"

"Your arrows," said Lutalo.

"What about them?"

"Take one out and shoot it and you will see what I mean."

"What are you talking about? What do I need to shoot at? There's nothing here. I don't need to shoot anything," he said.

Lutalo smiled knowingly at Mason, like he had a secret. "Just trust me."

"All right, but this is pointless." Mason heaved the leather bag off of his shoulder and pulled out his bow and one arrow. "Where do you want me to shoot?"

"Anywhere."

"I'm not even sure how to shoot one of these. It's probably just gonna go like three feet." He rolled his eyes as he pick up the bow and arrow and stared at it. He had never shot one of these things before. He tried to remember how he saw it done on *Tom and Jerry,* an old-fashioned cartoon he never told his friends he still liked to watch on DVD.

"We'll see," said Lutalo.

Mason began to grow frustrated. He didn't understand what Lutalo meant or what was going on. He raised his arms and took aim straight ahead. He was surprised at how light and natural the bow and arrow felt in his hands.

"Now shoot!" said Lutalo.

Mason obliged and released the arrow. To his amazement,

the arrow flew far ahead of them, farther than either of the two could see, leaving a glowing, yellow stream of light behind it.

"Whoa!" Said Mason. "It's like … magic or something."

"Yes. And now your arrow has led the way for us," said Lutalo.

"Way cool." Mason was now amazed and smiling. "Well, what are we waiting for? Let's follow the arrow!". The two boys raced after the yellow beam, with Mason in the lead and Lutalo close behind.

4

AFTER SEVERAL MILES, THE LIGHT BEGAN TO grow bigger and brighter and turn blue.

"I see the arrow!" Shouted Lutalo.

The arrow was stuck in a colossal tree. Its trunk was so wide that neither of the boys could see around it. Its roots were thicker than elephants' legs; they twisted around each other, forming beautiful swirling designs. The tail end of Mason's arrow was sticking out of one of the roots, shining alternately all the colors of the rainbow.

"Whoa … " Mason stepped forward staring at its magnificence, speechless. He stood in its shadow, as Lutalo moved up and stared at him. Both boys felt great awe and respect for this enormous sight.

"What is that thing?"

"Ah, you have no such trees back home?"

"We have giant redwoods in California. I've never seen

them though. This is heck of amazing!"

"Nature has many gifts, yes."

Mason stood quiet for a moment and then turned to Lutalo. "So, now what?" said Mason.

Lutalo was pensive. "I do not understand. The arrow was supposed to lead us to the Zebra. Why has it taken us to a tree? Maybe it was supposed to land on the other side of it. Wait here and I'll check."

Lutalo hurried around the base of the tree, looking for any clue that could tell him where they should go or what to do next, but found nothing. He stood perplexed.

"There is nothing here! This can't be right," he said, rounding back to Mason. "We have come such a long way and have been led to nowhere." Lutalo sank down onto one of the tree's giant roots to think.

Mason sat next to him quiet. He began to picking at debris on the ground, waiting for Lutalo who sat quietly thinking. When Mason could stand the silence no more he spoke.

"Maybe we did something wrong."

"No, not wrong."

Silence hung in the air between them again. Mason's boredom made him anxious and he started looking around. He tapped Lutalo. "Hey! Look up."

Lutalo came out of his meditative thought. "What?

"Look up."

"I can't look up! My father is gone and so is our Zebra!"

"No, I mean *look up* … at the top of the tree."

Lutalo slowly raised his head. Up high among the branches he saw a tiny tree house.

"We've done it! We've found what we needed to find."

"Yeah, but how are we going to climb up it?" Asked Mason.

"Oh. I had not thought about that. It must be 30 feet up," said Lutalo.

"Wait a second. The arrows! We'll use them as steps, like a ladder." Mason pulled the rest of his arrows from his bag. "Here, give me a boost up to this one."

Lutalo lifted Mason onto the arrow that had led them to the tree. Carefully balancing, Mason stabbed three more arrows into the giant trunk, one by his waist, one by his shoulder, and one far above his head. Pulling himself up to the next arrow, he called back to Lutalo.

"Start climbing behind me."

"I can't. You have to go up a little farther," Lutalo shouted back.

Mason climbed higher with the arrows, giving Lutalo a few more steps. Lutalo pulled himself up onto the bottom arrow, grabbing at the vines that hung from the tree branches to steady his balance.

"Now you'll need to hand me the bottom ones so we can keep going," said Mason. Lutalo clung to the vines, bending down to wrench the arrows from the tree. The two continued climbing for a very long time, with Lutalo handing up the bottom arrows to Mason. Halfway to the top, Mason stopped and stared at a small spider monkey that had been watching them. The monkey suddenly leaped from its branch right onto Mason's back.

"Hey! Look out!" Shouted Mason.

The monkey crawled down Mason's leg and jumped down onto Lutalo's head.

"Get off, monkey, you'll make me fall!" Cried Lutalo.

The furry little creature wiggled onto Lutalo's back and clung to him like he wanted to go for a piggy-back ride.

"Dude, cool he's taking a ride," said Mason looking down at the two of them.

"Well, he can't have one," said Lutalo, trying to shake the monkey loose. "Shoo! Get off."

The spider monkey grabbed onto one of the vines hanging next to it and scurried quickly all the way to the top of the tree.

"Wow! Wish I could do that," said Mason as he watched the monkey swing off into the jungle.

After a few more hours of climbing, the two boys finally reached the top and pulled themselves onto the dense, branch-covered front porch of the tree house. The structure looked large enough to fit about four kids inside. Mason reached out and knocked on the undersized, circular front door. Without any answer from inside, the door opened on its own.

The boys both stared in amazement. "Cool," said Mason with big eyes. "Should ... should we just go in?"

"Carefully," answered Lutalo in a cautious tone.

The two boys crawled, one at a time, through the tiny opening. As they stood up inside, they were astonished at the size of the place. What had looked like a simple, child-sized tree house from the outside was actually an enormous mansion inside. Clusters of bright yellow, orange and purple flowers protruded from the walls and ceiling. Lush, green moss blanketed the floor to make a soft and cushy carpet. Butterflies fluttered through the room like floating jewels.

"Wow! This is amazing," whispered Mason.

Lutalo was awestruck. "Yes," was all he could reply.

"Greetings," said a deep voice. Mason and Lutalo looked toward the opening of a hallway in the center of the far wall. There stood a tall, African man wearing a white linen sheet that wrapped around his shoulders and waist, reaching all the way down to his knobby knees. Deep wrinkles covered every visible inch of his skin, and his hair was whiter than fresh snow. He stood supported by a long, white, knotty walking stick.

"My name is Akili*," the old man continued, "and you two must be Mason and Lutalo. I wondered when exactly you would arrive."

"Y-yes," said Mason. "Um, how did you know who we are?"

"Oh, I know all about you and why you have come. You are looking for the Zebra of Life." Akili's voice was warm and calm, and made both Mason and Lutalo feel safe.

"Yes, and my father too," said Lutalo.

Akili smiled. "I know. I'll help you find them, but first you must eat and drink something and rest as well." Akili walked over to a large table in the corner of the room. "I suspect you both must be hungry after such a long climb up here. I hope you like what's here."

Suddenly a small feast appeared on the table. Mason stared in shock at the appearance of the food. Lutalo seemed hardly phased by the magic. Lutalo immediately sat down and plowed into the food like a starving lion. Akili grinned with kindness at Mason and gave him a gesture toward the table. "It's okay," he asserted. Mason hesitantly sat down. He watched Lutalo eat with such vigor and picked up his fork. His hunger overcame his reluctance, and he dug in and slowly began devouring the food with the same veracity as Lutalo. As they stuffed their cheeks full of hot and delicious foods, Akili continued speaking.

"You two have completed the first of many obstacles in your journey to find the Zebra and Lutalo's father. The first was finding me."

"What do you mean many obstacles?" Asked Mason with his mouth full of some kind of banana dessert that was covered in a warm, sweet, syrupy sauce.

"I know you will be able to find what you seek, and that a few more challenges stand in your way."

"If you know how to find the Zebra of Life and Lutalo's father, then why haven't you gone after them yourself?" Asked Mason.

Akili widened his eyes and laughed. "Do you really think an old man like me is capable of such a feat? How do you think I would have handled the climb down? My knees would never have permitted it."

"Oh, yeah," said Mason, as he glanced at Akili's old, worn knees.

"So what's next?" Asked Lutalo.

"You shall see, won't you," answered Akili with a knowing, but gentle smile.

"What!?" The two boys said in unison.

Akili laughed again. "You two have already solved one part of this puzzle without any help from me, which proves to me that you are capable of completing this journey on your own. But don't worry. You'll find help whenever you seek it. It may not be obvious to you, but trust me: The help you need is there."

Mason and Lutalo looked at each other, both feeling a little confused. "You will understand. And now I think you two should rest before you set back out on your quest. You may sleep there." Akili pointed to two exceptionally large lumps of moss, shaped like oversized easy chairs, which seemed to be growing out of the floor.

Mason and Lutalo shuffled over to the moss beds, completely full from their meal, and exhausted from their journey. They both tumbled comfortably into the soft, spongy mass and fell into deep, dreamless sleep. Akili smiled at his two slumbering new friends and left them to rest.

Mason later woke, not knowing how long he had slept, but feeling as if it had been for days. He looked over at Lutalo, who was just waking up himself and yawning. Mason stretched and wiggled out of his comfortable bed.

"Morning," he said to Lutalo.

"I can't remember when I have slept better," said Lutalo.

"I hope you slept well my young friends," said Akili, as he emerged from the hallway. "Now that you are ready to continue your quest, I have something to give you. This sack of food will help feed you and give you strength while you journey onward."

Mason placed the bag of food into his satchel and nodded his head as a thank you. Akili reached into his linen garment, pulled out a small stone statue of a man and handed it to Lutalo. "Give this to your village's leader once you return from your trip. He will know what to do with it. Take this cloth and wrap it up tight, you don't want to damage the statute."

"What is it?" Asked Mason.

"It looks like you," Lutalo said to Akili.

"It's a secret — for now," replied Akili.

"What isn't a secret with this guy?" Thought Mason.

Akili winked at Mason as if he had heard his thought. Mason's cheeks grew a little red, and he wondered how Akili may actually have heard him.

"Come now," said Akili. He walked back into the hallway, and the two boys followed him out onto a balcony behind the tree house.

"I don't remember seeing a balcony when we climbed up here," said Mason.

"We couldn't see very much of this place when we climbed up," joked Lutalo.

"This is where the rest of your journey begins, boys," said Akili. "Good luck, and remember that as long as you believe it you will always find help."

Mason and Lutalo looked out over the edge of the balcony and were reminded of how high up they actually were.

"But wait, Akili, how do we get down?" Asked Mason with his head still peering over the edge.

"He's gone," said Lutalo.

Mason ran back into the tree house, searching every corner for Akili. He was nowhere to be found. "Where could he have gone?"

Lutalo just shrugged.

"Well, how are we supposed to figure out how to get down from here?"

Mason placed his hands on his hips and frowned. Suddenly, two large, very long vines floated down from among the tree's leaves overhead, dropping at the boys' feet. Mason's eyes brightened and his frown disappeared. "Hey, Lutalo, have you ever heard of bungee jumping?"

"No? What is bungee jumping?"

"We're going to jump down and swing out of here."

"What!? You can't be serious!"

Mason gave Lutalo a wide smile as he grabbed the vine. "Trust me."

5

MASON GRABBED ONE OF THE THICK, GREEN VINES AND BEGAN wrapping it around Lutalo's waist and right leg.

"Oh, that's too tight!" Objected Lutalo.

"Sorry." Mason loosened the vine around Lutalo and wound it firmly around his right foot. "How's that? Is it still too tight?"

"No, that's much better. Thank you." said Lutalo.

Mason threw his satchel of bow and arrows over his shoulder and tightly secured it. He then twisted the other vine around his own waist and leg, and fastened their ends to the railing of the balcony. "All right, Lutalo, are you ready?" He asked, trying to sound confident.

Lutalo's eyes were as wide as silver dollars. He gulped hard, looked once more over the edge of the balcony, and nodded to Mason. The two of them climbed over the railing and Mason started counting.

"Ready? One, two, thr—."

"WAIT!" screamed Lutalo. Mason was so startled that he nearly lost his grip on the railing. "I can't do it," Lutalo whispered.

"Why?"

"I'm scared." His eyes drifted down, and he held tighter than ever.

Mason understood. Part of him hesitated too. He sighed and grabbed Lutalo by the shoulders. "Look at me." Lutalo's eyes stayed fixed. "No, me not the ground. Just take a deep breath and close your eyes. We'll jump together."

"Okay."

"On three we'll jump. One, two, three!"

Lutalo squeezed his eyes shut. Mason pushed them away from the edge of the balcony and began to slowly soar down and forward.

"Lutalo, open your eyes! We're flying!" Mason whooped. Instead of plunging toward the ground, the boys were gliding through the air as if they were strapped to an invisible trapeze. Mason was overwhelmed by the beauty that surrounded him and Lutalo. He imagined they were swimming through a peaceful, green ocean filled with reefs of colorful flowers, schools of glittering bugs, and herds of elephants spouting like whales under white waterfalls.

Lutalo released the fear and managed to open his eyes. His expression rapidly changed from fear to excitement. "Woohoo!" Shouted Lutalo.

Mason looked over at Lutalo and saw him gripping his swinging vine with one hand, rearing his head backwards, and smiling even bigger than little Sebahive. Mason immediately burst out laughing from seeing Lutalo's newfound excitement. "This is great!" He bellowed.

"I knew you would like it!" Mason shouted back as he continued to scream with laughter and adrenalin.

The two of them floated from vine to vine through the jungle for what seemed like miles, and at last came to a soft landing at the base of a mountain. Mason's heart was beating fast, as if he felt a spider was tap dancing inside his chest.

"That was amazing," he exclaimed, jumping around in a circle. Suddenly he stopped. "Now what?"

"I'm not sure," said Lutalo, still happily reeling from the adrenaline rush.

"Well, it won't be as fun as swinging through the jungle like Tarzan."

"Like who?" Asked Lutalo.

"Never mind," laughed Mason as he caught his breath and looked around. "Where do you suppose we are?"

"I think we are standing somewhere on Mount Kilimanjaro," said Lutalo, as he took in their new surroundings.

"What!?" Mason yelled. He smiled in disbelief. "Mount Kilimanjaro! How? I mean, how could we have swung that far?"

"It doesn't matter," Lutalo interrupted. "Let's keep moving."

They began to slowly navigate their way up the mountainside, past strange vegetation, giant boulders, and over the craggy ground. Lutalo, leading the way, stopped abruptly and held up his hand to Mason.

"I see something down there", he whispered." Pointing to a black truck with a horse trailer attached to its bumper. It was being driven just a few miles ahead of them around the foot of the mountain. "It's them! It is the men who took our Zebra of Life. It's their truck!" Lutalo growled quietly.

"Are you sure?" Asked Mason.

"I'm sure," answered Lutalo. His face was filled with misery. "We'll never catch up to them. They have a truck and we're on foot, and they are miles ahead of us."

"Don't worry. I have my arrows. " Mason reassured Lutalo as he pulled off his leather satchel and took out the bow and an arrow with a recently acquired expertise. "I'll shoot this one at their tire to slow them down for a while." He held up the bow with a new confidence, fixed the arrow into place, pulled back, and released. The arrow punctured the truck's left, rear tire.

"Yeah!" Mason exclaimed. "High five!" He said, as he held

up his hand. Lutalo frowned at the foreign gesture, smiled and shrugged. Mason, who was now amused, grabbed Lutalo's hand, "Now slap it!" He coached Lutalo, who smiled, nodded and obliged — only much too hard.

Mason tried not to laugh a little as he shook the sting out.

They watched the truck come to a swerving stop, waited until its doors opened, and four men stepped out.

"I can't see my father," said Lutalo.

"Maybe they don't have him."

A few minutes later, a fifth man stepped out of the truck. He looked like a tower of strength. Even from far away, Mason could see that the man's dark skin was as smooth as velvet; it stood out from his light clothing. He wore a white, collared, button-up shirt, khaki shorts and brown shoes that looked like leather tennis shoes. His wrists and ankles were bound together with rope.

"Father ..." whispered Lutalo with an almost breathless joy to see his father again. Mason looked over to see a tear roll down Lutalo's cheek.

"We'll get him back," said Mason, placing his hand on Lutalo's shoulder.

He and Lutalo watched as all the men scrambled around the truck, trying to figure out what had happened.

"Let's go," said Lutalo.

"Right behind you." Mason jumped up and raced down

after Lutalo, who was already yards ahead of him.

They hurried as fast as they could down the mountain, around more huge rocks and slippery inclines. As they rounded a massive boulder, an enormous, black panther suddenly leaped in front of them. The boys skidded and fell back as they froze in their tracks, paralyzed by fear. The giant cat's eyes glowed like bright spotlights shining on each of the boys, and its fur shone in the sun as if it were wet. The panther's muscles bulged with every step it took toward them. Its enormous paws were bigger than Mason's own head.

"One swipe and I'm dead!" He thought.

The panther began circling Mason and Lutalo. Mason and Lutalo squeezed in close together. "What … what do …" Lutalo grabbed his arm. "Nothing," he whispered. "Stay still." The panther moved in closer — and they could feel its hot breath on their skin. They shuddered in pure fear, as the huge feline pushed its way between them, knocking Lutalo to the ground. Mason reached his hand out to his fallen friend, but felt too scared and weak to pull him up. The panther circled out wider, as if to give the boys some space, then stopped abruptly in front of them.

"You will never catch up to those men if you continue on this path," it said.

Mason's and Lutalo's jaws dropped.

"Don't be afraid," the panther continued.

Lutalo gulped down some of his fear. "You're not going to … eat us?" He asked; his chest was still heaving in terror.

The panther narrowed its eyes and seemed to smile at them. "Well, I am little hungry. I wasn't fed a feast like the two of you had at Akili's."

Mason gasped in surprise. "How did you know about Akili's?"

The giant cat purred, sat on his hind quarters, and licked his paws in a nonchalant, smug kind of way. "Oh, I know a lot about the two of you," it purred as it took one last lick.

"But, but … you're a panther," replied Mason

The panther moved up into Mason's face, which reflexively made Mason pull backward and peer cross-eyed down his nose as the great cat's glistening eyes narrowed on him. "And your point …?" he asked looking right into Mason's eyes.

"No … no point," Mason stammered back.

"Good. Now, I know a shortcut. It's through this mountain. If you come with me now, I'll show you a way to get ahead of those men." The great panther got up and started walking. Both boys started, and the cat whipped back around and growled, "Now!"

Mason came out of his shock. With his fear slowly subsiding, Mason finally helped Lutalo to his feet.

Lutalo stepped forward. "Lead the way."

"By the way, my name is Jelani*," said the panther over his shoulder, as he dashed back around the boulder.

6

THE BOYS CREPT CAREFULLY BEHIND JELANI, still a little wary about trusting a wild, talking beast. Jelani stealthily and easily climbed ahead of them and hardly seemed to notice that they might struggle on this uneven terrain. The boys just kept moving and didn't complain.

"I guess this is what Akili meant," whispered Mason.

"Looks that way," Lutalo replied, not looking at Mason, but keeping his eyes on their jet-black leader. He noticed Jelani was beginning to move faster over the mountain's rocky terrain. "Come on, faster," he called back to Mason.

Lutalo sprinted after the cat as Mason struggled to keep up. He dashed from rock to rock with ease, while Mason tried his best not to slip after each step. Soon Lutalo and Jelani were far ahead. Mason grew nervous. He was falling too far behind. He thought he would never be able to catch up to their speed.

"Wait!" he shouted. Jelani and Lutalo quickly made their way back to the small rock Mason had plopped down onto. "I … need a … a break … and some water," he huffed and puffed. "Dude and I thought I was rockin'! You guys kill me," he breathed hard.

Lutalo frowned at him. "Rockin'?" The slang escaped him.

Jelani made a strange kind of growling noise, which the boys figured was his way of laughing. He once again sat on his hind quarters to nonchalantly lick his paw as he spoke. "American boys … all skateboards … motor bikes … bicycles … little real exercise," he stopped licking and gave Lutalo a look. "Now here …," he slinked up to Mason, "we use our muscles," and rubbed up against and around him, wrapping his tail up his arm. "Every day," he purred and tapped Mason's bicep with the tip of his tail.

Mason curled up the right side of his mouth, giving his two companions a crooked smile. "Maybe I should join a gym!"

Lutalo knew nothing of gyms and shrugged. Jelani, though, started laughing with that same familiar growl. He untangled himself from Mason. "You do that …," he said as he sauntered away.

Mason was self conscious now and looked down at his bicep. "Yeah … that's what I'm gonna do," he declared with a newfound resolve.

"Uh-huh," said Jelani with a tinge of skepticism. "Let's keep going — water ahead." Jelani continued walking.

"I'm thirsty too," said Lutalo.

The three of them continued up the mountain with Jelani leading the way, making sure they stuck close together. They suddenly came upon a group of trees that seemed to have sprung up out of nowhere. Mason was amazed that such lush greenery could grow out of hard and rocky ground.

"Just behind those trees ... fresh water," said Jelani.

"Are you sure?" Lutalo asked. "I can't hear any sounds of water."

Jelani looked back at the boys and smiled. "Trust me," he said.

Mason dashed past Lutalo and ahead of Jelani, straight into the grove. He darted past a few trees, through several vines, around a large shrub, and then stopped abruptly in his tracks. "Lutalo, Jelani, come quick!" He yelled. He stood for a moment in amazement. There before him lay a glistening pool, with water as clear as glass, and a sparkling, white waterfall with a vivid rainbow shining out from behind it. Mason then felt a hard thump on his back.

"I thought you said you couldn't run that fast," said Lutalo, as he gave Mason another quick slap on the shoulder.

Mason gave an open-mouth smile. "I'll race you to the water!"

"Wait! You're not supposed to drink the water without boiling it first," warned Lutalo.

"Hey, Jelani," said Mason, "I thought you said this was fresh water. Lutalo says we have to boil it first."

Jelani once again made his low-growling noise and licked his nose. "This water is completely safe and delicious."

Mason dropped his satchel of arrows, quickly kicked off his shoes, and pulled off his shirt and socks as they rushed toward the pool. Lutalo shouted and whooped as he jumped right in. The two gulped down the cool refreshing liquid by the mouthful, while Jelani stet down by the side of the water, leisurely lapping at it. They took turns standing under the waterfall, swam and splashed, and Mason taught Lutalo how to play Marco Polo. The two of them were having so much fun that they nearly forgot about the purpose of their journey.

After swimming for what seemed like hours, the boys noticed Jelani slowly rise from the side of the pool. "It's time we got moving again," he said in his soft and gentle voice.

Mason and Lutalo swam to the edge of the pool and crawled out. Mason put his shirt, socks, and shoes back on while Lutalo hunted around the trunks of the trees.

"What are you doing?" Asked Mason.

"Looking for the statue Akili gave to me. I set it down under one of these trees — ah ha! Found it," he cried, as he raised it high over his head to show Mason. "Hey, where is Jelani?"

Mason looked around for the panther, but he was nowhere in sight.

Suddenly, Jelani appeared along the other side of the pool carrying something in his mouth. He dunked the object into the water then brought it over to the boys.

"What are those for?" Asked Lutalo.

"Ehwaya fayoo," Jelani mumbled, with two thick bamboo sticks in his mouth.

"What?" Mason asked.

"Waya fayoo!" Jelani practically choked trying to speak. Mason and Lutalo doubled over laughing at his attempts. The panther dropped the sticks at the boys' feet.

"I said it's water for you."

"Oooooohhh," the boys cried in unison.

"Yes, you can carry water with you in these bamboo sticks."

"That's great," said Mason, "thanks, Jelani."

"Yes, thank you," said Lutalo.

"Now come on. We've still got to hurry," Jelani said as he quickly swirled around and headed back into the trees.

•   •   •

Meanwhile, back at the base of the mountain, Mwamba and the Zebra watched as their kidnappers tried desperately to extract the golden arrow out of their truck's tire. So far, none of the men's efforts seemed to be doing any good. One man in particular, who was extremely short but had bicep muscles the size of bowling balls, had tried pulling on the arrow for an entire hour. After claiming that the task was impossible, another man, with a blonde mustache that curled up and touched the sides of his nostrils, suggested that they tie a rope to the arrow and all pull on it at once. But even with all four of the men straining against the small weapon, it still would not budge. The men eventually grew frustrated and angry with each other. They shouted and spat at each others' new suggestions. Mwamba couldn't help but chuckle at how silly they all looked and sounded.

•   •   •

Mason, Lutalo and Jelani had not gotten far when Lutalo yelled for them all to stop.

"What's wrong?" Asked Mason.

"The statue, the one Akili gave me, it's gone. I must have dropped it back at the pool."

"Dude, man ... that's a long ways back."

"Too bad," sighed Lutalo.

"Hurry!" Jelani ordered.

Rushing back to the giant pool, Lutalo tried to remember where he had first found the statue, and where he might have dropped it. He quickly searched the edge of the pool, but found nothing. Then he spotted it, lying in front of a patch of bushes. As he reached down to grab it, a crocodile the size of a school bus lunged out from beneath the bushes and snapped at Lutalo's hand. Lutalo gasped and fell onto his back, stunned. The crocodile wiggled toward him, snapping his snout full of razor-sharp teeth. Lutalo immediately sprang to his feet and slowly backed away from the croc as it stared and hissed at him.

"Oh!" Lutalo whispered, too scared to shout.

The crocodile held still for a moment, and then clamped its jaws shut and slowly slithered back into the jungle's brush. Lutalo snatched up the statue and grinned.

"That was easy," he said. He turned to head back to meet Mason and Jelani, but instead found himself staring right at them. Jelani was posed like he was ready to pounce, his muscles bulging, eyes glowing like fire, and fangs showing. Mason sat crouching behind the arching black cat. "Oh! I thought I ... but it was you," Lutalo stuttered, a little embarrassed.

"Dude, *really?*" Mason laughed, "Get real."

Lutalo slapped Mason's arm just a bit. "I guess not."

"Yeah," Mason rolled his eyes.

Jelani strolled up and bumped Lutalo, "Yeah!" He glanced back over to where the croc had backed off.

"Friend of yours?" Asked Mason.

"Trouble ... always trouble. So, I thought I should come along ... just in case. He doesn't like me," Jelani smirked.

Mason and Lutalo laughed together. "You think ..." Mason smiled.

"Now this time make sure you both have everything you need; we can't be delayed any further," Jelani stated firmly.

"Right," the boys assured him together.

The three travelers once again hurried away from the secluded pool, more energized than ever, and headed up toward a large ridge. As they scaled the wide rim of the mountain, Mason could see another unusual patch of greenery.

"How is it that anything can grow on these rocks?" He wondered.

Jelani walked straight into the shrubbery and disappeared.

"Hey, wait!" Shouted Lutalo.

"Come on in," Jelani called, his voice echoing.

Mason and Lutalo pulled away some of the plants and discovered Jelani sitting in the mouth of a cave.

"This is a shortcut," said Jelani as he again disappeared into the dark cave. As they slowly entered, Mason and Lutalo began to feel nervous and stayed close to each other for protection. It was pitch black inside the cave, and they could no longer see Jelani. Mason reached out for Lutalo and managed to grab his shoulder.

"I can't see anything, and it's freezing in here," said Mason, squeezing Lutalo tighter. The air inside of the cave made the boys feel like they were trapped inside of a giant ice cube.

"Maybe try an arrow," Lutalo answered and nudged Mason.

"Oh, cool. Yeah," said Mason as he reached into his satchel and pulled out an arrow. As he searched for his bow; the arrowhead sparked and ignited.

"Whoa!" Exclaimed Mason, holding the new torch as far away from him as he could.

"Great! Let me have one too," said Lutalo.

Mason handed Lutalo another arrow, which immediately lighted itself. They continued deeper into the cave for what seemed like miles and noticed that there were drawings on the cave's walls. Lutalo saw one that looked like the crocodile he had met by the pool. Mason looked up and observed that the roof of the cave appeared to be moving.

"Lutalo look up," he said.

"Shhhh," whispered Lutalo, "those are bats. Let's not wake them up." Mason nodded in agreement, and then suddenly tripped, dropping his torch, and falling to his hands and knees. He looked back to see what had caused him to stumble and saw what he thought was a bunch of white sticks. Lutalo held his lighted arrow up to the objects to examine them. Both boys' eyes widened and their jaws dropped.

"Bones!" Lutalo yelled. His voice echoed through the cave, waking the swarm of bats. The walls of the cave seemed to rumble as a shower of black wings rained down from the roof of the cave, slamming into the boys' faces and scratching their skin.

"Let's get out of here!" Mason shouted. He grabbed his arrow-torch as Lutalo yanked him up by the arm. The boys sprinted straight ahead.

"I can see some light," shouted Mason, with bats still swirling around him. They ran even faster toward the end of the tunnel, tripping over each other until they finally fell to the ground and rolled out of the cave, landing at Jelani's front paws. The bright sunlight instantly warmed the boys and calmed them down.

"Are you all right?" asked Jelani.

"Yes, fine" Mason panted.

"Good. Now be quiet and follow me." Jelani crept between two nearby boulders and instructed the boys to quietly join him. Mason and Lutalo squirmed together behind the panther and peered down at the kidnappers' truck where the men were still struggling to pull the arrow out of the tire with a rope.

"Listen, I can hear them fighting," Lutalo whispered.

"You idiot! You gave me rope burn," growled the short man with huge biceps.

"Well it's not my fault if you have sweaty hands," shouted another man, who was bald and wore giant sunglasses with green lenses.

The man, who stood at the back of the group, still hanging onto the rope, had long, greasy black hair. "Hey you!" He called to Mwamba. "Come try and get this arrow out." Mwamba rose to his feet and hobbled over to the flat tire. He bent down to examine the damage then lifted his head and smiled.

"What is it? What are you smiling about?" Barked the man with the curly mustache.

Mwamba stretched his smile even wider and raised his eyebrows at the man. "Only the one who shot this arrow can take it out. You must change the tire."

The men bugged out their eyes and looked back and forth at each other. "Why didn't you think of that!?" They all screamed.

As they continued to bicker, Mwamba twisted his head around looking for the source of the arrow and continued to smile knowing that his son was behind it.

Lutalo stared at his father with a small smile on his face and his eyes wide, glowing with pride. "That's my father." Lutalo then lowered his head. "He should never have let those men stay over," he looked down, shaking his head.

"What?" Asked Mason.

"Father invited them to stay over … and now look."

Jelani read the disillusionment on Lutalo's face and came over. He took his tail and wrapped it around Lutalo's shoulders to provide comfort. "Good men have good hearts. Would you have expected him to turn away men in need? Optimism and trust are good things, Lutalo. Don't be disappointed in him … look upon evil as evil. And besides, life is an adventure … you took an adventure and you met Mason — and most importantly me," chuckled Jelani.

Lutalo's expression brightened. He lifted his head. He understood that Jelani was right, but still couldn't help feeling a little disappointed in his very human father. "I just want everything to be back to normal again," he said in a quiet voice.

Crouched down across from Lutalo, Mason leaned forward. "Hey, dude, it's fine. My Dad does dumb stuff all the time … but you know what! He's my dad. You gotta love your Dad. Look how you turned out. I mean hey! Who else is going to be brave enough to jump off cliffs and climb steep mountains with no water like an idiot, huh?"

The two friends laughed at what on the face of it sounded crazy. Lutalo looked to Jelani and gave him a smile too. "See Lutalo … it's all good," said Mason as Lutalo nodded, and both boys turned their attention back to the situation below.

7

MASON ROSE TO HIS FEET. "I want to get a little closer to those men. I can't hear them unless they're yelling."

"All right, but be careful — and quiet," warned Jelani.

Lutalo nodded in agreement with the panther.

"I will," reassured Mason.

Mason crept between two large, nearby rocks and into a patch of dried-up brush located right at the front of the kidnappers' truck, where he could hear every word the men said. Mason suddenly felt a sneeze coming on. He clapped his hands to his face and stifled the sneeze, but rustling the bushes in the process.

Mwamba quickly looked to the bushes where Mason hid, and then back toward his captors to check if they had heard the rustling too; but they were all too busy changing the tire. Looking back to the brush again, he could see Mason's face peering from behind the dried-up vegetation. Mwamba nodded and motioned for Mason to stay put; but with his hands bound, Mwamba looked as though he was signaling for Mason to come out. Mason took a deep breath, stood up, and stepped out into the open.

Lutalo became terrified as he and Jelani looked on.

"What's he doing!?" He whispered frantically. "He's going to get everyone killed!"

"Wait," Jelani quickly cautioned.

Mason slowly walked toward Mwamba. He felt like he was in a daze. He wasn't sure exactly what he was going to do — and he was beginning to regret revealing himself.

"Hey, there's a kid!" Shouted the man with the greasy, black hair.

All four of the men turned toward Mason and stared at him. The man with the curly mustache smiled at Mason, exposing a mouthful of rotting, brown and yellow teeth. He stepped out from behind the other three and began to walk toward Mason.

"Are you lost, boy?"

"No," said Mason with an edge of defiance.

The man with the mustache smiled even wider and chuckled and nudged his friend. "Well, looky here. We got us one of them spoiled American brats." He shoved Mason who fell back a bit and was now officially nervous, but kept his cool.

Mason composed himself and nodded toward the back of the truck. "What's in the trailer?"

"Well, that's really none of your business," said the man, as he twirled one of his mustache curls.

Mason stood straight up, refusing to back down. He had a plan. "I … I'm sorry. Hey look, I just need a ride … please."

The curly-moustache man grinned and nodded. "Now that's more like it. You be asking us nice and all — yeah, we'll take you back. Just let us fix this here flat tire."

"Thank you," said Mason in a flat tone, figuring it would give him a chance to speak to Mwamba.

"That's a good little boy."

Mason cringed at being called a little boy, but smiled at the man and took a seat next to Mwamba.

"Are you okay?" He whispered.

Mwamba widened his eyes and nodded.

"Hey what's in the trailer?" Mason shouted again to the kidnappers. "And why is this man tied up?"

The man with the green-lens glasses stepped out from behind the truck. "That man there … he's a thief and a liar. We're taking him to the proper authorities."

"What did he do?" asked Mason.

The man dabbed at the sweat on his forehead with a red bandana and leaned forward, sneering at Mason. "You're a pushy little feller, ain't you."

The "little" stuff was starting to get on Mason's nerves. He took a deep breath and leaned forward, leaning on his elbow. "Hey!"

The man now curious cocked his head to hear better, "What you want now?"

"I'm 14. I'm not 'little' or a 'feller'. I'm from America. And where I come from you get a fair trial. People don't just haul you off to jail unless it's in the back of a cop car — and they have good cause."

"That so … well you ain't in America anymore boy. And what our friend here done is between him and us. So keep your nose out of it or you can just walk your butt on home!" He turned and spit on the ground and stepped back behind the truck.

Mwamba seized the moment and whispered, "I know that bag you have … it's my son's."

Mason nodded and his eyes sparked as he sat up a bit. He had forgotten he was carrying the bag and the arrows. "If those men knew what was in this bag we'd be in big trouble," he said.

"Do you know my son, Lutalo?"

Mason smiled at Mwamba. "Yes."

"Where is he? Is he okay?"

Mason nodded toward the rocks where he had left Lutalo and Jelani. Mwamba's face brightened as he looked over.

Mason and Mwamba suddenly heard the men speaking to each other, but couldn't see them from where they sat.

"There. It's fixed. If we leave now we can make it to the boat by tomorrow's sunset," said one.

"What about the boy?" Asked another.

"Forget the boy. Let's move!"

All four men came strutting out from behind the truck. The man with greasy, black hair grabbed Mason by the wrist and yanked him up from his seat.

"Hey, watch out," shouted Mwamba.

"Shut up and get in the truck," said the short man with muscles.

Mwamba glared at him and did what he was told. He climbed into the truck, followed by the kidnappers. Mason anxiously stood by and watched as they loaded themselves in.

"Hey, wait! Where are you going? Aren't you gonna give me a ride?" He asked.

"Sorry, boy, no room," said the driver, curling his mustache again.

"I can't let them get away again," Mason thought. "Hey! Don't forget your tire," he shouted. Mason walked over to the tire and pulled the arrow out with ease.

"Did you see that!?" Screamed the man with huge biceps. "That kid just pulled the arrow out of the tire!"

"What!?" Yelled the other men together. They stuck their heads out of the truck's windows to see Mason holding the arrow up and grinning.

"Grab him!" Shouted the mustached man.

Mason sprinted back toward the bushes and disappeared between the rocks. The man with the curly mustache looked on as the other three kidnappers sprang from the truck and ran after a Mason. As they were about to enter the bushes, Jelani leaped from behind the rocks, growling and swiping at the men. They screamed and froze in their tracks.

"Nobody move," said the man with greasy, black hair. Jelani paced back and forth in front of the bushes, blocking their way to Mason and Lutalo.

"Just back up slowly," gasped the man with green-lens glasses. The men began to inch their way back toward the truck. Jelani turned and faced the men and let out a fearsome, threatening roar. "Panther!" One man shouted, as the three men screeched and fell all over each other as they scrambled and ran back to their truck.

"Start the truck! Start the truck!" Shouted the man with green-lens glasses, waving his red bandana in the air.

The three men jumped into the truck, rolled up the windows, and locked the doors.

Mwamba rocked back and forth, laughing at how scared they were. "I've never heard three grown men scream like little girls before," he cried.

The three men panted and sank into their seats.

"What about the boy?" Asked the driver.

"Forget him. Go!"

Mason and Lutalo looked on as the men sped away with Mwamba and the Zebra.

"Are you all right?" Lutalo asked Mason.

"Yeah, I'm fine," Mason panted.

"How is my father? Is he hurt? He's okay, yes?"

"He's fine. But those men said they are taking him and the Zebra to a boat somewhere."

Jelani quickly trotted up to the boys. "I think I know where they are headed," he said. "Wait here; I'll be back in a moment."

As they watched the truck vanish out of sight, Lutalo stood silent. He was frustrated and turned to Mason, "Now what? I'll never see my father again," he complained.

Mason looked him right in the eye with complete certainty. "Mom taught me to think positive no matter what."

"How can I feel positive now?" Retorted Lutalo. "They're long gone."

"Because you have no choice … you want your dad back? Then do it! They'll be plenty of time to regret stuff later."

Lutalo looked longingly at the dust cloud kicked up by the truck speeding off into the distance. He nodded, sighed and squeezed his friend's shoulder. "Thank you for making me feel better."

Mason nodded. "You're welcome."

Lutalo looked around. "Where's Jelani?" He asked.

Mason handed him one of the bamboo canteens. "We should drink some water. We need to be ready to move when Jelani comes back. Speaking of Jelani ..." Mason said, as the cat came rushing up to them.

"Let's get a move on," said the cat. "The kidnappers are headed for the Nile, but they will have to stay on the road and take the long way there. We can beat them if we take the way through the valley. That's the quickest route to the Nile."

"The Nile River!" Shouted Mason. "I'm gonna have to cross the Nile? Isn't the Nile the longest river in the world?"

"Yep," Jelani and Lutalo said together.

Mason stared at them. Now it was his turn to think positive. He rose to the occasion, swallowed hard and nodded. "Okay!"

All three companions nodded at each other.

"Follow me," said Jelani.

8

MASON AND LUTALO SPED AFTER JELANI FOR SEVERAL HOURS. As Jelani looked back at his two followers, he noticed their tired and worn-out faces.

"It's just a little ways more, boys, and we can have a break," the panther shouted back to them. "Can you see that stream up ahead? We're almost there."

Mason and Lutalo stumbled up to the edge of the stream, panting and sweating. Mason took the bamboo canteens out of his satchel.

"Let's fill these with water," he said, as he handed one to Lutalo.

Lutalo waded out into the stream, balancing himself on the large rocks at the bottom of the water. As soon as he was waist deep, his right foot slipped out from under him, and he was instantly dunked under. Mason howled with laughter. Lutalo bounced up and shook his head, stunned from the coldness of the water.

"Hold on," Mason extended his hand, "let me help you."

Jelani strolled over to see if the boys needed help. Mason leaned over the edge of the water and stuck out his hand. Lutalo reached up and gave it a hard jerk. Mason let out a yelp and grabbed at whatever he could to steady himself. Jelani tried to dodge out of the way, but he was too late. Mason gripped onto the panther's tail as they both were pulled into the water. Mason and Lutalo laughed and watched Jelani quickly spring back onto dry land.

Jelani quickly began lapping his coat and shaking off. He indignantly looked at the boys. "Panthers *don't* like water," he proclaimed and shook off more water. The boys eyed him and smirked. Jelani just peered down his nose as he licked his fur, paused and stopped. "Well ..."

"Well what?" Asked Mason.

"Don't just stand there and stare. You're wet too. We'll need to dry off and stay the night."

The boys nodded in unison. They stripped down and out of their clothes down to their skivvies, and then diligently hung their wet clothes on a nearby tree. Jelani snuck up behind them and one last time shook out his soaking, wet fur, getting the boys wet all over again.

"Hey!" They protested.

"That's for pulling me in!" Jelani said with a wide smile.

"Now, let's build a fire."

The boys didn't hesitate. Mason gathered up some dried twigs into a pile. He pulled out one of his arrows and touched its tip to the wood. The pile sparked and ignited into a full flame. Lutalo lined the edge of the fire with rocks as Mason pulled out the brown sack of food from his satchel. The three travelers settled themselves around the warm flame.

"This is nice," said Mason. "I don't really get to camp much. I could get used to this. My mom is a hotel camper. She likes to go on trips all over, but she only likes to stay in hotels. She doesn't like the dirt, she's scared of bugs, and she has to have a clean place to shower, but most of all she has to have her fresh coffee." Mason looked up and saw the first stars of night coming out. "I do miss home. I've been gone a long time. I'm glad we're getting to camp like this, though. Now the only thing missing is my best friend Cole and my guitar."

Jelani could see that Mason missed home and wanted to cheer him up. "What's in that bag?" He asked.

"Oh, yeah, let me check!" Mason reached into the bag and pulled out a giant slice of pizza. "Whoa! No way!" Mason smiled at Jelani. "Want some?" He asked, as he waved the slice in front of the panther.

"No, thanks. Already ate."

"When?" Asked Lutalo.

"I found something when I was checking on the kidnappers' route."

Mason took a bite of the pizza. "Don't tell me what it was," he said with his mouth full. "I don't want to hear it while I'm eating." He reached back into the bag and pulled out a slice for Lutalo.

Lutalo wrinkled up his face. "This doesn't look very good."

"Just try it, you'll like it. I don't know anyone who doesn't like pizza."

Lutalo stared at his piece of pizza for a moment then took a small bite. He widened his eyes and looked at Mason. "Hmm!"

"I told you!"

Turns out, a whole pizza pie was hidden in that bag. The two boys each ate four slices. Mason reached back into his bag after his fourth slice.

"I wonder if there's any dessert in here," he said as he pulled out a handful of chocolate chip cookies. "Oh, you're going to love these too, Lutalo."

After finishing their dinner, the boys and Jelani gathered some leaves and made themselves soft, cushy beds. Before they could even finish saying goodnight, both boys were fast asleep.

The next morning, Mason and Lutalo woke to find Jelani missing.

"Where could he be?" asked Mason.

"I'm not sure. Let's clean up and refill our canteens. Maybe he'll be back by the time we're done." Lutalo stood up and headed over to the stream.

Mason reached into his sack of food for some breakfast and pulled out a peanut-butter-and-jelly sandwich.

"Lutalo! Come here quick!" He shouted. His friend sprinted over from the water.

"What!? What is it?" Lutalo yelled.

"This is my favorite sandwich. You've got to try it."

"Mason! Don't do that. I thought you were hurt or something."

Mason laughed. "Oh, chill out and try it. I'll bet Jelani will be back by the time we finish breakfast."

"You're probably right. Now let me try that sandwich. If it's half as good as the pizza then I know I'm going to love it." Lutalo sat down next to Mason and took a giant bite out of his first peanut-butter-and-jelly sandwich. He closed his eyes. "Mmmmmm, it's good," he said. "Hey, do you think Jelani is out having his own breakfast right now?"

Mason looked like he was going to be sick. "I'm not going to think about that," he shuddered. "I don't want to know what Jelani is eating, and I don't care as long as it's not me," he said with a slight chuckled.

Jelani came rustling through a patch of tall grass with a

smirk on his face.

"Hey, you two, let's get a move on," he shouted.

Lutalo snatched up his canteen and stone statue. "Ready."

Mason shoved his bag of food into the red satchel and hopped up. "Me too."

"The valley is just beyond those hills," said Jelani. "Let's go."

Mason and Lutalo raced as fast as they could up the slopes of the hills.

"I'll bet I can beat you to the top!" Shouted Lutalo.

"You're on!" Said Mason.

Suddenly Lutalo burst forth at a speed Mason didn't even think was possible for a kid to do. He looked on as his friend scurried up to the top of the hill, and then stopped dead in his tracks. Mason was panting heavily as he slowly reached the top of the steep slope and clapped his friend on the back.

"You win," he huffed and gently slapped his friend's back.

"SHHH! Don't move!" Whispered Lutalo.

Mason looked down at the bottom of the hill to see a pack of grazing wildebeest.

"Don't scare them or they will stampede," said Lutalo.

Jelani calmly walked up behind the boys. "What's wrong?"

"There's a pack of wildebeest down there," answered Mason.

Jelani let out a chuckling growl. "You should see the sight

of you two … scared stiff," chided Jelani. "Those wildebeest won't be spooked by us. In fact, I had a talk with them this morning, and they agreed to be your transportation."

"Transportation?" Asked Mason.

"Yes, come with me," said Jelani.

The three of them walked down the hillside and up to the nibbling animals.

Jelani looked at the boys and nodded toward the wildebeest. "Pick one," he prodded in earnest.

The boys looked at the panther, both confused.

"What? Just hop on top of one of them?" Asked Lutalo.

"Sure, they're very friendly, and they won't mind."

Mason crept skillfully up to one of the animals and patted its neck. "Nice wildebeest," he said as he climbed onto its back.

Seeing his friend climb easily onto the animal's back made Lutalo relax a bit. As he climbed onto another wildebeest he looked over to his friend and said, "Look here. Mine's bigger," he smugly declared.

Mason didn't take the bait. "Ah so what."

"So, are you boys ready?" Asked Jelani.

Mason and Lutalo hugged onto the thick of the animals' necks.

"Ready," replied Mason.

Jelani looked to each of the wildebeest, who nodded

back to the panther, signaling they were ready, too.

"Then let's go," said the panther as he sprinted off into the valley.

The wildebeest quickly took off after him. Mason tightened his hold on his animal's neck and looked over to his friend, who was doing exactly the same. The wind smacked against their faces as the wildebeest ran faster and faster after Jelani. The animals traveled so fast that the scenery around them became a green-and-yellow blur. Mason's stomach tickled as if he were on a roller-coaster ride. His wildebeest began to slow its pace as they neared a group of gazelles. Mason adjusted his balance as he looked up to see them resting next to a pool filled with gi- ant, soggy water buffalo. Once the wildebeest had passed the other animals, they swiftly picked up speed again.

After what seemed like hours, Lutalo called out to Jelani.

"My butt hurts!" He complained.

"Yeah, mine too," chimed in Mason.

"We're almost to the edge of the valley. Just a few more miles," Jelani shouted back.

Within a few minutes, the wildebeest finally came to a stop and lowered themselves to the ground, letting their passengers off. Lutalo hopped off his ride as Mason stumbled off.

"My legs feel like jelly, but that was way cool!" He said as he gave Lutalo a high five.

"Not like swinging through the jungle, but close," said Lutalo.

Mason quickly spun around and cupped his hand to his ear. "Can you hear that?" He asked. "It's the roar of the river! We made it!"

Jelani lowered his head toward the wildebeest and thanked them kindly for their help.

"It was no trouble at all, and thank you for not eating us," replied the larger of the two wildebeest. "Good luck to you."

The smaller wildebeest nodded its head and winked at Mason and Lutalo, who smiled back and watched as the two animals galloped back to their herd in the valley.

"Boys, come over here," said Jelani. "Take a look." Jelani stuck out his neck, indicating for the boys to look into the distance.

Far ahead, as far as the boys could see, a working village lined both sides of the Nile River. There were countless small huts squished together, and numerous boat docks anchored all sizes of boats from small ships to barges and ferries. Several of the huts had store fronts that opened up to the water, with food, fishing nets and boating supplies for sale.

As the three of them headed toward the village, Jelani quickly stopped.

"Look there," he said. "Do you see the truck and the trailer? It's headed for the village."

"Are you sure it's theirs?" asked Lutalo.

"Yes."

As he spoke to the panther, Lutalo couldn't help noticing that Jelani looked a little sad.

"Jelani, are you all right?" He asked.

"I'm fine. It's just … well, never mind."

"We made it. We found them," said Mason. "And we're ahead of them!" He squinted to watch the truck as it sped toward the river, leaving a thick trail of dust in its tracks. "It looks like they're headed for the river dock where that big red and blue boat is."

"That's not just a boat; it's a barge," said Lutalo.

"What's the difference?" Mason asked.

"A barge is more for hauling heavy stuff down a river. It's not like a passenger boat that people ride for fun." Lutalo watched the truck pull up to one of the docks. "Look. The people are clearing off the dock. They're making room for the truck and trailer."

"So, what do we do now?" Asked Mason, looking to Jelani.

The panther looked at the two boys and smiled somberly. "I'm sorry, boys, but this is where we must part."

"What!?" The two boys shouted.

"I have come as far as I can with you. You know I don't like water. The two of you will be fine."

Lutalo swallowed and felt sad. He walked over and gently scratched behind Jelani's ears. Jelani purred in delight. "Thank you for all of your help, Jelani," Latalo said. "We never would have made it this far without you. I thank you, my village thanks you, and my father thanks you." He gently petted the panther's back as Mason slowly approached them.

"Hey … um … thanks," said Mason. He laid a hand on Jelani's head and scratched behind the other ear.

"Over to the right a little," Jelani purred.

The three friends embraced for a few more moments in silence.

"Come now, boys, it's time for you to get a move on," said Jelani.

"You leave us first," encouraged Lutalo.

Jelani rubbed up against Lutalo and Mason, as if to give them a goodbye hug. "Until we meet again, my friends," he said and dashed back toward the way they came.

The two boys watched Jelani disappear from sight.

Mason gave a quick sigh. "Well, let's not waste time."

Lutalo nodded to his friend. "Let's go."

9

B USY VILLAGERS BUSTLED ALL AROUND THE
BOYS, some directed boats into the docks while
others sent them out onto the river. A massive, white fishing boat with a horizontal, green stripe around it slowly
floated toward one of the empty docks. Huge nets full of
fish were piled all across the boat's deck. To Mason and
Lutalo it looked as though nearly all of the villagers were
rushing up to the giant boat. A small section of the mob
quickly began to tie and anchor the boat, while another
group helped empty the loaded fishing nets and immediately started gutting and cleaning the fish. Once the small
group of villagers had secured the boat to the dock, they
hopped onto the deck and began mopping and cleaning
the rest of it.

"Good day fishing," said Lutalo admiring the catch.

Mason nodded.

A thick, muscular man stepped off the boat. He smiled broadly and stuck his thumbs through the belt loops of his pants. "Good work everyone," he shouted. He chuckled to himself and showed that he was missing his two front teeth.

"That must be the captain," Lutalo observed.

"He looks happy," Mason commented, trying to get a better look.

"With that load … of course. Bad day … the crew's doing all of the cleaning on the boat."

"We should sneak on the barge now … while they're distracted," said Mason.

The boys quickly slipped past the crowd of cleaning villagers and snuck behind a wall of metal cages filled with different kinds of small monkeys and birds. As they were passing, a spider monkey sitting in one of the cages grabbed at Mason's satchel, nearly spilling out his arrows. Lutalo quickly shooed the monkey's hand away and steered Mason forward by his shoulders. They stepped out from behind the cages, up to the side of the barge and right next to the black truck.

"All clear," Mason whispered. "You go first — quick!"

"Are you sure? Do you see the kidnappers?"

"No, I don't see any of them. Just duck down under the truck's windows. If any of them are in there, they won't see us."

Lutalo squatted down, and then walked past the truck. Lutalo slowly and carefully began to climb up the side plank of the barge. Mason started to grow anxious. They had been out in the open too long and Lutalo was going too slow. He rushed up behind his friend and pushed him onto the deck.

"Whoa — hey, why are you pushing?" Asked Lutalo, looking shocked at Mason.

"Sorry, sorry, sorry! I didn't mean to push. I'm just really nervous."

"Well then let's find somewhere to hide."

They boys immediately spotted a huge pile of wooden crates in a far corner of the barge's deck. They quickly crawled behind the stack and, sitting comfortably hidden, they waited for the kidnappers.

Mason wiped the sweat from his forehead. "Whew!"

"I can't believe it. Any minute now my father's going to be on this very same boat with me."

"Just remember to stay quiet when we see him. We can't let ourselves be noticed."

"Don't worry."

"Shhh … listen — I think they're backing the truck onto the barge now."

The boys peeked through a space between the crates. About a dozen people were hurrying around the deck, talking and loading things onto the barge. The rear wheels of the truck's trailer drove into the boys' view, followed by the rest of the trailer and the black truck. Its doors then swung open and out stepped the four kidnappers. The man with the green lens glasses pulled two blue tarps from the back seat. The man with the long, greasy black hair helped him spread one over the cab of the truck, and the other over the trailer to cover the zebra.

"Look who it is!" Whispered Mason.

The captain of the white-and-green fishing boat walked up to the men and began talking.

"What's he saying?" Asked Lutalo.

"I don't know."

The man with the curly, blond mustache handed the captain a crumpled wad of money. They nodded to each other and the captain walked out of the boys' view.

"Ha ha! We sail in two hours, boys!" shouted the mustached kidnapper. "Let's clean up and get some food."

They slammed the doors of the truck shut and left.

Mason and Lutalo sat quietly for a half an hour, watching the captain's crew finish loading the barge until they finally left too.

"I think it's safe for us to move," said Lutalo. He carefully moved aside one of the crates and stuck his head out into the open. "Everyone's gone. We can get out."

Mason crawled behind his friend into the open space of

the deck. Lutalo scrambled on his hands and knees over to the truck then stood up. He quickly pulled back the blue tarp and saw his father; bent over in the back seat with his hands tied to his ankles. Lutalo frantically pulled on the door handle.

"Father!" He yelled.

Mwamba turned toward the window. He blinked and shook his head for a moment then gave a huge open-mouth smile. "Lutalo!" He cried, his voice muffled through the window glass.

"The door is locked!"

Mwamba wiggled himself closer to the truck door and lifted the lock open with his teeth. Lutalo jerked open the door and threw his arms around his father.

"Father!" He shouted with joy. "Are you okay?"

"I am wonderful now that I have my boy with me, but I'll be even better once I get these ropes off me."

Lutalo tugged and pulled at the ropes, but they wouldn't budge.

"Mason, come quick."

Mason hurried up to the truck door.

Mwamba smiled at him. "It is good to see you again."

"You too," said Mason smiling back. He quickly pulled out one of his arrows from his satchel and began using the head as a knife on the thick ropes. The ropes were soon cut through, and Mwamba pulled them off from his wrists and ankles.

"So you are *the one*," said Mwamba looking wide-eyed at Mason. "You are the one who shot the arrow — the one who flattened the tire." Mwamba ran his fingers over the arrow, admiring its beauty. "It is my understanding that they only work for good. So, you my friend must be good." He stepped out from the truck, stretched for a minute, and headed toward the back of the trailer.

Lutalo helped his father move away the tarp. Mason gripped onto the trailer's handle and tried to lift it up. "Uuuugggh — it won't move!" He grunted.

"Let me try," said Mwamba. He gave the handle a hard shove and managed to slide it up.

Mason and Lutalo stood back while Mwamba opened the door and climbed in. He slowly stepped toward the zebra and began petting its neck as he whispered something into its ear. The zebra then backed out of the trailer, allowing Mwamba to be its guide.

Mason marveled at the sight of the zebra. It was like no zebra he had ever seen before. He had seen some at the zoo and on the Discovery Channel, but this one was far more majestic and impressive than all the others. The zebra had a large, stocky build, and a huge head with cute, rounded ears, all attached to a thick neck lined with a shiny, upright mane.

The stripes of its coat were wide and glossy — and its black hooves supported strong, muscular legs.

"It's beautiful," Mason thought to himself.

Suddenly the zebra swished its sleek tail and hit Mason on the head.

"Not another mind reader," he laughed.

Lutalo looked a little confused at Mason. "We'd better get going," he said.

Mwamba grabbed a rope from the back of the truck and tied it around the zebra's neck.

"Now, remember to act calm among the villagers. We don't want to attract attention," said Mwamba. The boys nodded.

The four of them casually walked off of the barge with Mwamba leading the way. "Which way did you come from?" He asked.

Mason pointed up to the right. "Just beyond those trees. There's a big valley behind them." He sighed. "I was ready for a ride on the Nile, but I guess there's no chance of that now. I was ready to ride some rapids, see some hippos, maybe even an anaconda — that would have been good and scary!"

As the four of them walked on, they admired all of the goods displayed in the shops. Nearly all of them had whole, dried fish hanging from the ceiling. Some had jewelry and crafts set up on tables. Mason wanted to get something for his mom, but he didn't have any money. He felt a little nervous when a few of the merchants stopped and stared at him. Mason knew he was standing out with his sandy blond hair. "Is he for sale?" He heard someone ask. One of the villagers had approached Mwamba and was asking after the zebra.

Mwamba smiled at the man. "No, not this one. I am going to use him as a mule to help plow my fields."

The villager gave a short bow to Mwamba and walked away.

"I hope no one else notices the zebra," said Mason, "especially the kidnappers."

"Can you see them anywhere?" Lutalo asked his father.

"No, I don't see any one of them."

The four of them picked up their pace. They hurried out of the village and through the entrance to the valley.

"Let's find a spot to hide and take a break," said Mwamba. "I need some water too, and maybe I can find some food."

They soon came across a colossal tree with giant roots sticking out of the ground, which made a sort of fort for them to crawl into. Mwamba tied the zebra to one of the roots and told it to lie down and rest, which it promptly did. Mason and Lutalo crawled under the roots and made room for Mwamba.

"Stay here, boys. I'm going to see if I can find some water and maybe a bit of food."

"Wait a minute," said Mason. "We have both here."

Mwamba cocked his head to the side and gave Mason a puzzled look. Mason took off his satchel and reached in for his food bag. He pulled out the bag and handed the satchel to Lutalo, who then took out the bamboo canteens.

"Here, it's water," he said, handing a canteen to his father. "Is there any pizza still in there?" He asked his friend. "I want my father to try it too."

Mwamba gave the boys another confused look. "Pizza?" he asked.

"Yes, pizza. Mason gave me some from this bag. I didn't think it looked very good, but I was so hungry that I tried it and it was so delicious. You'll like it."

"Well if you say so," said Mwamba. "By the way, this is a pretty clever idea, making canteens out of bamboo. How did you think of that?"

Mason and Lutalo looked at each other and smiled.

"Um, it's sort of a long story," answered Lutalo. "We didn't actually think of it ourselves, but I'll tell you about it later."

"It looks like the zebra is getting his fill of food out there," said Mwamba.

The boys looked out from behind the tree roots and saw the animal peacefully lying down and nibbling at the grass around it.

"It sure is a beautiful zebra," said Mason.

Mwamba nodded. "The most beautiful in the world. And now how about that pizza?"

"Oh, right." Mason pulled out a big slice of pepperoni pie and handed it to Mwamba, who was so hungry that he nearly swallowed the piece whole. As he chewed on the new food, his eyes lit up.

"Mmmm, son, you were right. This is quite delicious." Mwamba ate a whole five pieces before he was full.

"Boy, you must have been hungry," said Lutalo. "I've never seen you eat so much."

Mwamba patted his stomach and smiled. "Now, boys, we'd had better be going. I'm sure those men are soon going to realize that the zebra and I are gone. And I have no doubt that they will come after us."

"Why do they even want the zebra?" Asked Mason.

"I heard them say something about selling it to a research company in America. But I'll tell you more about it later. Right now we must leave." Mwamba crawled out of the root fort and began to untie the zebra from the tree. "They were planning on taking me to the authorities and lying to them about me to get me killed. I'm sure if they catch us, they'll do something worse."

• • •

Meanwhile, back at the barge, the man with the mustache listened as the little man with muscles bragged to the crew about their big plans for the zebra. With the blue tarps still covering the truck and trailer, they remained oblivious to the fact that their captives had escaped. The man with the mustache held a plate of food and picked at it here and there. He was growing tired of the big talk from the little man with big biceps. He had also taken a liking to Mwamba and felt a little sorry for eating while his innocent prisoner starved. He walked over to the truck to give Mwamba his leftovers and lifted away the tarp. He gasped at the sight of the empty truck and dropped the plate, shattering it and splashing food all over the deck. He rushed back to the trailer and ripped off its tarp. Empty. He waved the tarp over his head and slammed it to the floor. "Calm down," he said to himself. "Mike! Come here."

The small muscle man was in the middle of telling a story to some of the crew members. He waved his hand at the mustache man, indicating for him not to interrupt.

"Mike, come here!" He said forcefully.

Mike rolled his eyes and stepped over. "What's your problem?" He whispered, embarrassed by his associate's behavior in front of the crew. "What's so important that you can't wait five minutes for me to finish telling a story?"

"Every minute I wait is another minute we'll be behind Mwamba and the zebra. They're gone!"

"WHAT!" Mike screamed. "Get this truck off the barge! NOW!" he shouted to the crew. "James! Go get Reynolds and Smith!" The man with the mustache ran off the barge to find his fellow kidnappers. Mike kicked at the boxes and crates blocking the truck's way off the barge. "Get this crap out of my way in 10 seconds!" He yelled. "Anything still in my way after that is getting run over!" He jumped into the truck and peeled off the barge, smashing loads of supplies that the crew had failed to move in time. The other three kidnappers came running up to the truck, waving their arms and shouting for him to stop. Mike slammed on the brakes to let the men pile in then speed off again.

Smith, the man with the green lens glasses, spoke up. "One of the villagers said they saw a man with two kids and a zebra heading back toward the valley. He said one of the kids had yellow hair."

"Golden arrow boy," whispered Reynolds, the man with greasy black hair.

"We'll go faster without the trailer," said James. "Smith, Reynolds, unhook it. I don't want the zebra anymore. I want those arrows."

•   •   •

Mwamba finished untying the zebra from the tree. "I'm sure those men will find our tracks. They are professionals."

He whispered into the zebra's ear, took the rope off of its neck, and sent it off running.

"Hey! It's running the wrong way," said Mason.

Lutalo folded his arms, smiled and nodded in approval. "Father has a plan, don't worry."

Mason watched the zebra run through the valley. In its wake, the valley's grass and foliage seemed to flourish and turn even brighter shades of green, and sprouted new flowers and plants.

"See?" nodded Lutalo toward the zebra's trail in the distance. "Look at how lush and green the valley has become from the zebra's very presence."

"But why didn't it work before? When we were walking out here nothing happened."

"The zebra is smarter than you think. I'll bet that had something to do with what my father whispered to it. It probably works like the arrows — only for good. If it had used its powers before, then those villagers would have noticed — and we would have been given away for sure."

"Look," pointed Mason. "It's coming back."

The zebra trotted up to Mwamba, who gently placed the rope back around the zebra's neck.

"Let's go," said Mwamba.

As they walked, the ground beneath the zebra stayed the same, not flourishing, not dying either.

"I get it now," said Mason. "The kidnappers will think the zebra is running around free in this valley somewhere. They'll probably stop and look for it and give us time to get ahead."

"Precisely," said Mwamba.

10

"STEP ON IT, MIKE!" JAMES GROWLED. He pulled at his mustache as he scanned the landscape ahead of them, looking for any sign of their group's prey. "Everyone look. Keep your eyes peeled for anything. If you see so much as a pile of dung, tell me — anything that might give us a clue to where they are."

"I can't see anything, Boss," said Reynolds.

"Yeah, me neither," added Smith.

"I mean it! *Do not* even blink," James roared back. "Mike! What are you doing? I told you to step on it!"

"Boss, look." Mike slowed the truck to a stop and pointed straight ahead. "I think those are tracks."

"Everybody out! Check those tracks, they could be theirs! Not you, Mike. You stay in the truck. Be ready to take off as soon as we come back."

"You got it, Boss."

James, Smith and Reynolds quickly hopped out and ran to the front of the truck. All three squatted down and inspected the ground, picking at the grass, and looking for similar nearby marks.

"Look at the pattern they make. These tracks lead straight toward that valley," Smith observed.

James twisted a lump of grass between his fingers and put it in his mouth. He chewed and furrowed his brow.

"What is it, Boss? Is it them?" Asked Smith.

James narrowed his eyes and smiled, showing the grass stuck in his teeth. "Jackpot." He sprang to his feet. "Let's go, boys. Mike, we're leaving!"

"Where're we headed?" Asked Mike, as his three companion kidnappers leaped back into the truck.

"The valley straight ahead."

The four men sped toward their targets, anxious and on the edges of their seats, straining to see as far ahead as they could for any glimpse of Mason, Lutalo, Mwamba and the Zebra. They soon entered the mouth of the valley.

"Boss, are you seeing this?" Asked Mike. "Look at this valley. It's greener. It's fertile. It's not the same as when we went through it before."

"They must be here. Stop the truck. Everyone spread out and look for them. Meet back here in one hour, with or without them."

The men fanned out for clues. Mike headed toward the left into a thick group of trees, covered with even thicker layers of vines. He swung them out of his way, tripped over them, pulled at them, and waged a mini-battle with one particularly long and tangling vine, momentarily forgetting to look for his victims' tracks.

Reynolds ran northeast for a few yards, and then dropped to his stomach and crawled through the newly sprouted vegetation, checking every suspicious-looking blade of grass. Smith veered right, scrambling from shrub to bush, sniffing and licking their leaves. Unfortunately, one of the bushes was poisonous; his tongue immediately began to swell and blister, leaving him howling in anger and pain. James went northwest examining the ground for any items the boys or Mwamba might have dropped. After an hour of searching in vain, the men met back at the truck.

Reynolds slammed his hat on the ground and shouted. "I don't believe this!"

"I din't fine anthy,'" mumbled Smith.

"What did you say?" asked James.

Smith stuck out his swollen tongue. James, Reynolds and Mike stepped back in shock.

"So, what you're saying is you didn't find anything either?" Mike asked the bubbly-tongued Smith. Smith shook his head.

"I don't know what happened. The zebra has obviously been here. The valley is full of new grass and plants that were not here yesterday. They have to be …" James stopped speaking, dropped his head down, and began to laugh wildly. The three other men looked at one another, confused and a little nervous.

"What's so funny, James," asked Mike.

"Boys, we've been duped!" He cackled.

"Ha ya me?" Asked Smith. Drool spilled from the corners of his mouth.

James laughed harder. "Smith, don't even bother talking. No one can understand a word you're saying. Those boys and Mwamba have tricked us. They must have had that zebra work its magic around this spot and knew that we would stop to check it out. By now they're hours ahead of us."

"So now what!?" Yelled Mike.

"Let's head back to the village. Later I'll call in a helicopter. We'll be able to spot them easily if we're above them."

"Who do you know who has a helicopter?" Asked Reynolds.

"Don't worry about that. All we need to worry about is finding those guys and the zebra."

11

"LUTALO, LOOK OVER THERE. It's that same pack of wildebeest from before. Let's see if they'll give us a ride again."

Lutalo lit up with excitement. "Father, come quick, we have found ourselves a ride across the valley." He grabbed his father's hand and hurriedly dragged him and the zebra toward the tame pack of animals.

"Uh, hello," Mason timidly said to one of the wildebeest. "Do you remember us? Two of you gave us a ride through the valley a while ago." The beast just stared back at Mason and loudly chewed a mouthful of grass. "Um, we were with a black panther last time, Jelani. Do you remember us at all?"

"Well of course," said the animal, spilling some of the chewed up grass out of its mouth.

"Oh," said Mason, a little shocked. "Well, could you give us a ride again? We're in a bit of a hurry."

"Absolutely! It will be our pleasure."

Lutalo, Mwamba and the zebra walked up beside Mason and the wildebeest, who gave a slow, short bow to the magical creature. The zebra winked back.

"Any one of us will give you a ride," said the wildebeest to Mason.

"You boys pick one and I'll ride the zebra," said Mwamba.

Each of the humans quickly mounted an animal. Lutalo informed the beasts that they needed to go all the way to Mt. Kilimanjaro. All three animals nodded and immediately sped off, with the zebra leaving a full blooming trail of greenery and flowers in its path.

The wildebeest and the zebra raced doubly fast back through the valley, all the way to the foot of the mountain, and then came to an abrupt stop. Mason slowly slid off the back of his ride. His legs shook beneath him from gripping onto the animal's torso.

"Whew! Thanks for the ride," he said. The sound of his voice went up and down as he tried to regain his balance.

"Yes, thank you again," said Lutalo with the same dizzy lilt in his voice. Mwamba hopped off the zebra.

"You're welcome. Be safe. And do everything you can to protect the Zebra of Life." The two wildebeest gave one last bow to the magical animal then trotted away.

"We'd better start hiking," said Mwamba. "We can't

waste any time." He suddenly looked surprised at Mason and his son as they began chuckling together. "What is so funny?"

"It's not going to take as long as you think to get past this mountain," answered Mason.

"What? Why?"

"Because, Father, we know a shortcut — through the mountain!"

"How?"

"A talking panther showed it to us," his boy answered matter of fact.

Mwamba, in disbelief, placed a hand to his forehead. "Uh … um, lead the way."

The boys ran to the hidden opening in the side of the mountain where they had rolled away from the storm of angry bats.

"Here!" Shouted Lutalo, pointing into the tunnel. "It's right here."

"Well what do you know? There really is a secret tunnel. But, Lutalo, it is pitch black in there. How are we to get through if we can't see where we are going?"

"Not a problem," said Mason. He pulled an arrow out of his satchel and handed it to Mwamba. He took the weapon in his hand and stared at Mason, entirely confused. "You have to light it first," Mason continued.

"I just don't understand," Mwamba shook his head.

"Here we'll show you," said Lutalo. Mason took out two more arrows and handed one to Lutalo. As both boys stepped into the darkness of the tunnel, the arrows sparked into flame just as before. "You see, Father? Now let's get going."

"Watch out for bats," Mason joked.

Mwamba's own arrow immediately lighted itself after he and the zebra stepped into the tunnel. "Amazing," he whispered.

The four travelers hurried through the mountain, carefully avoiding the piles of bones and bugs, until at last they came to the edge of the jungle on the other side.

•   •   •

"Everybody in!" Screamed James. He waved Smith, Reynolds and Mike into the roaring helicopter. They each strapped on their seatbelts and a headset, and James gave the signal to take off. "Head for that valley," he instructed to the pilot.

Flying over, they saw the fresh, wide swath of lush vegetation leading up to Mt. Kilimanjaro.

Reynolds anxiously tapped on the window of the chopper. "What happened? Where are they? The trail just ends."

"Fly around to the other side," ordered James.

Still nursing his swollen tongue, Smith grunted at the sight of the trail on the opposite side of the mountain.

"I see it, Smith," said James. "They must have found a way through the mountain then headed into the jungle." He clenched his fists, half furious half pleased. "Let's land."

• • •

"It's getting pretty dark, boys. We'd better set up a camp for the night."

Mason, Lutalo, Mwamba and the zebra crawled under the shelter of a fallen tree trunk. Its inside was hollowed out and was big enough for all of them to sit comfortably underneath it. Mason pulled out his brown food bag again, and they each had a turkey sandwich, and more than a few brownies. As they ate, the boys told Mwamba of their journey to find him and the zebra, and about Akili and his tree house. They talked and talked until all four of them finally fell asleep.

"Everyone, be quiet," whispered James. The four kidnappers had been watching their prey for hours, waiting for a chance to make a move. "Mike, you and I will get Mwamba. Smith, Reynolds, once we have him you two get the zebra. Leave the boys."

The men nodded to their leader and all four silently crawled toward the camp. James was the first to reach Mwamba. He pulled a large bowie knife from his belt and held it to the man's neck. "Wake up," he whispered.

Mwamba slowly opened his eyes and jerked at the sight of his kidnapper. James pressed the knife closer to Mwamba's neck. "Shhhhh! Don't fight or we'll kill you and the boys." Mwamba nodded. James motioned for Smith and Reynolds to grab the zebra. The four men silently led their two prisoners away from camp, leaving the sleeping boys under the log.

12

MASON AND LUTALO WOKE EARLY IN THE MORNING.

"Where are they!?" Mason shouted.

"No! No, this can't be happening again! Those men must have come here in the middle of the night, and they took my father and the zebra again." Lutalo moaned and buried his face in his hands.

"Wait a minute. Maybe we're wrong. Maybe your dad just took the zebra to get a drink or something."

Lutalo lowered his hands to reveal frustration and anguish. "No. My father wouldn't leave us. I know *those* men took them again."

Mason stayed calm — he needed to think. "The trail, the trail!" He sprung up with excitement and hit his head on the roof of the hollow log.

"What are you talking about? What trail?"

"The zebra's trail!" Mason answered, rubbing the top of his head. "The zebra had to have left a trail behind it. We can follow it."

Lutalo gasped. "Let's go!"

The boys crawled out from under the log and promptly spotted the zebra's trail. They followed it for several yards, all the way to the bottom of a steep hill.

"We'd better be careful," warned Mason. "Who knows what's at the top of the hill. The kidnappers might have set a trap or something for us."

"Right, we'll go slowly," agreed Lutalo.

As they began to ascend the hill, James appeared at the top, holding onto his bowie knife and grinning menacingly. "Hello, boys."

Mason and Lutalo stopped dead in their tracks. "Give me back my father!" Lutalo shouted.

"And the zebra!" said Mason.

"I'll gladly give you what you want, but I'll need something in return," said James.

"What do you want?" Lutalo stepped forward with assertion — he was well past anymore fear — he was angry, outraged and wanted to jump on James and pound on him.

"Those arrows," James answered, pointing to Mason's satchel.

Mason and Lutalo looked at each other, both unsure of

what to do. "Give us a second," said Mason.

"Sure, sure, talk among yourselves," James chuckled.

"Mason, what do we do?"

"Give him the arrows."

"But what if the kidnappers try to trick us?"

"What if we tell him we want to make the trade closer to your village, outside of this jungle where we can see better?"

Lutalo nodded in agreement.

"Okay, we'll give you the arrows," Mason shouted up to James.

"Hand them over, and I'll give you Mwamba and the zebra."

"No."

"No?"

"No, not yet. We want to make the trade closer to Mwamba and Lutalo's village."

"What!" Said James. "Why should I do what you want?"

"We have the arrows, you want them — and we want Mwamba and the zebra. You don't trust us, and we don't trust you … seems pretty clear to me," said Mason who felt proud of his own cleverness and growing confidence under such stress. "Deal?"

James stroked his moustache, thinking it over. He relented, "fine."

"Meet us outside of the village at noon today."

"Wait a second now, I'm not going to get too close to that village. I don't want anyone recognizing me or my men. We'll go as close as two miles outside of the village."

"OK ... two miles," asserted Mason. Lutalo was impressed and looked with surprise at Mason.

"Yeah, yeah!" James waved them off and went on his way.

The boys hurried back to their camp to prepare for their meeting with the kidnappers.

"Let's eat something then head for your village." Mason pulled two warm blueberry muffins out of his food bag. "I think you'll like this, Lutalo."

"I'm not really hungry."

"You should still eat something."

Lutalo took the muffin and bit into it. "I can't believe how good all the food from that bag has been."

"Yeah, good stuff," Mason said through a full mouth.

"I feel better. Thank you," said Lutalo. "I'm just looking forward to getting my father back and this whole thing is over."

The boys smiled at each other and finished their breakfast in silence. They then immediately set out for Lutalo's village. Mason plunged through the juggle. Lutalo followed close behind, trying to keep up; but Mason had a newfound confidence and direction. He too wanted this over. He missed home and these guys were just getting on his nerves now. He moved quickly and pulled branches and jungle vines out of his way and held them appropriately for Lutalo to pass, and then he would pass him and continue. They soon arrived at its outskirts at exactly 12:00 noon.

"They're not here yet," said Lutalo. "What if they don't come at all?"

"Look! I see them. They must have followed close behind us."

The four men, Mwamba and the zebra came marching out of the jungle brush. Mwamba tripped as Reynolds jerked the rope tied around his wrists. Smith led the zebra by a rope as well, but no trail of blossoming flora followed the animal. Mason followed after Lutalo, who was rushing up to meet the men and animal.

"What have we here ... again," said James with a sinister smile. "Two little boys. Lutalo wants his *daddy* back," he taunted as he gave him boo-boo lips and wiped away a fake tear, mocking them.

"You're like cockroaches," hissed Mike. All four of the kidnappers chuckled.

"This isn't such a bad trade for us, you know," continued James. "We figured that we probably would have never been able to sneak the Zebra of Life out of the country. It will be easier to take the bow and arrows instead. So, hand them over."

"Not until you let Lutalo's dad and the zebra go," declared Mason.

James glared at the boys. He turned to Smith and nodded. "Just do it."

"But, Boss — I"

"Do it, Smith. Reynolds, you too."

The two men released their captives, who hurried over to the boys. Mwamba wrapped his thick, muscular arms around his son. He then looked at Mason and asked, "Are you sure you want to trade the arrows? Maybe we can convince them to take something else."

Mason winked at Mwamba. "I'm sure."

"All right, boy, we've given you what you want now give us what we want," said James. "I'm not going to ask again."

Mason pulled off his satchel and admired the bow and arrows one last time.

"I'll go with you," said Mwamba.

"No, I want to do it by myself."

"If you need help, yell."

"I will, but I think I'll be okay." Mason slowly walked up to the kidnappers, placed the weapons at James' feet, then turned and quickly walked away.

James snatched up the bow and an arrow. "Foolish boy," he said, and took aim at Mason's back.

"Mason, look out!" Screamed Lutalo.

Mason swung around as James released the arrow. The boy froze and could do nothing but watch as the weapon sped toward him like a lightning bolt. The arrow suddenly swerved to the right and began flying back at James. The man with the mustache leaped out of the arrow's way, landing on his stomach.

"Who is the foolish one?" Mason quipped. "Those arrows can only be used for good."

James picked up the bow and arrows that had now turned back into plastic toys. He glared at Mason; his face was flushed and filled with rage. "These may only be used for good, but this isn't." He dropped the toys, pulled out his bowie knife, and rushed toward Mason.

Suddenly Jelani raced out of the jungle, sped past the other kidnappers, and leaped onto James, pinning him to the ground.

"Jelani!" Shouted Mason.

The panther growled over James, baring his razor-sharp teeth.

"Help," squeaked James. "Somebody, help."

Smith, Reynolds and Mike stood still and refused to get close to the wild animal.

"I can call him off," said Mason.

"Call him off!" Cried James.

"You have to promise something first."

"Anything! Anything, just get him off me!"

Jelani drew his face closer to James', causing him to nearly faint.

"You have to promise to leave and never come back here again."

"Yes, yes …"

"Promise!"

"Fine! Fine! I promise."

The three other kidnappers shouted their agreement.

"Thanks, Jelani. You can get off him."

The black cat stepped off of the frightened mustached man, walked over to Mason, and sat down next him. Mason, Lutalo, Mwamba, Jelani and the zebra all watched as the men scrambled back into the jungle, leaving behind the toy bow and arrows.

Mason hurried to retrieve the toys. As he picked up the bow and arrows, they magically transformed back into their splendid, golden form.

"Lutalo, look, they're golden again!"

Lutalo smiled at his friend. Both boys then turned to their old friend Jelani. Lutalo squeezed the panther around its neck as Mason rubbed the cat's back and scratched its ears.

"Jelani, it's so good to see you," exclaimed Lutalo, with his voice muffled as he snuggled his face into Jelani's neck.

"It's good to see you both are safe," grunted Jelani. "Lutalo, not so tight!"

"Sorry!" Lutalo loosened his grip on Jelani and sat back on his heels.

"I see you've gotten the Zebra of Life back from those men," Jelani continued, giving the zebra a bow. "And is this your father, Lutalo?"

"Yes! Father, come meet our friend Jelani!"

Mwamba stepped toward the panther. "It is good to meet you. My boy and his friend have told me all about you. I can't thank you enough for all of the help you have given them."

"It was my pleasure," replied the panther. "These are a fine pair of young men, and I am proud to call them my friends. But I must leave you once again. I want to follow those kidnappers just to make sure they don't get any bright ideas and try to come back. Excellent work my friends, and farewell!" And Jelani dashed away after the kidnappers almost as fast as he had reappeared to them.

"Goodbye!" The three humans shouted.

13

WITH THE ZEBRA AND MWAMBA RETURNED and the kidnappers defeated, Mason and Lutalo could not have felt happier. The two heroes, rescued father and the zebra swiftly began their trek toward the village from where their whole adventure had started. As they walked through the village's rancid fields of crops and trekked through the barren, dry ground, the three humans witnessed the zebra's magic revive the land back to life. The limp, molded crops slowly began to rise.

"Look at the fields!" Cried Lutalo.

"They are becoming even more beautiful than before — so full, so rich!" Mwamba replied.

The brown-and-yellow colors that had covered the ground now dissolved into brilliant greens that stretched farther than any of them could see and grew almost up to their heads. With every step the zebra took, a trail of bright plants and flowers of every imaginable color sprouted from the ground. Mason, Lutalo and Mwamba could instantly smell the sweet scent of the blossoms.

"It smells like when my mom makes pancakes with lots of syrup — or poppy-seed muffins!" said Mason.

"It reminds me of the dessert we had at Akili's," added Lutalo.

"Lutalo, we are home!" Said Mwamba.

They looked ahead and saw a stream of villagers slowly pour out into the fields. Many fell to their knees and stretched their hands to the sky and let out gleeful "Yeah!" Several more embraced each other and apologized for their quarrels. Mwamba turned his attention to the boys and noticed that they too were dancing with joy. He placed a strong arm around his son's shoulder. Lutalo looked up at his father with pride and placed his own hand onto Mason's shoulder. As the three of them walked on, leading the Zebra of Life, the crowd of villagers ran up to them, one by one, shouting and cheering thanks and praises.

Mwamba led them straight to a large hut in the center of the village. Members of the crowd ran up to the hut shouting "Reth! Reth!"

"What is 'Reth'?" Asked Mason.

"You mean who is Reth?" Answered Lutalo. "He is our leader."

A round, old African man stepped out from the hut. He walked slowly with the help of a wooden cane that was decorated with elaborate carvings, jewels and shells. Mason marveled at his crown covered in a rainbow of feathers, beads and small animal bones. The top of the headdress reached at least two feet above the man's head. "How does he keep that from falling off?" Mason wondered. The old man walked gracefully toward the four new arrivals, grinning from ear to ear, which made the wrinkles on his face appear even deeper.

Mwamba and Lutalo bowed to the old man. Mason quickly bowed too.

"Sir, this young man is Mason," Mwamba said to Reth, placing a hand on Mason's head. "And you remember my son, Lutalo? These two are the ones who saved me and the Zebra of Life."

The old man gently petted the zebra's mane and smiled, and then turned to Lutalo. "I could never forget Lutalo," he bellowed and gave the boy a hug. Reth then grabbed Mason's hand, shook it violently, and let out a roaring laugh. Mason hardly had time to recover from the wild gesture before the old man pulled him in closer and gave him a kiss on both cheeks. "We must celebrate and honor the three of you with music and a feast! You have restored not only our village's most prized possession, but our whole village as well! You two, take the Zebra of Life to the fields! He needs to rest and eat." Two villagers immediately rushed up to the zebra. They stroked its back and tickled its ears, and then joyfully led the animal away to rest.

Shocked by the old man's playful spirit, Mason laughed and felt welcomed. He felt calm too, until he remembered something important. He tapped Lutalo on the shoulder and whispered in his ear.

Lutalo gasped. "Father!" Lutalo gently pulled his father's arm and leaned in close to his ear. "Mason and I need to do something."

Mwamba nodded. "Okay, but don't go too far."

"We won't."

The boys excused themselves and walked over to a nearby shady tree. They scrunched down and huddled their heads together. Lutalo pulled the wrapped statue from Akili out of his pocket. "Should we unwrap it or just give it to Reth?"

"I think we should just give it to him," said Mason.

Mason and Lutalo walked over to Mwamba and Reth, the king, who seemed to be deep in a conversation.

"Um, excuse me, Father ... and sir," he nodded to Reth. His voice quivered as he continued. "Sir, excuse me for interrupting, but I need to give something to you. When Mason and I first started our journey we met a man named Akili, and he wanted me to give you this." Lutalo held out the statue, still covered in its cloth. "I'm not sure what it is for or why he wanted me to give it to you. We haven't opened it, and we're not sure if it has been broken at all. We were told not to tell anyone that we had it. *'Sorry, Father.'*" Lutalo looked to his dad, smiled and shrugged his shoulders.

"No worries, my son."

Lutalo looked back at Reth. The old man was trembling as he took the small item from Lutalo's hands. "Y-you, met Akili?"

Lutalo nodded.

"My, my ... are you sure you did not look at it?"

"Yes, sir," he replied.

"Well, what better time to look than now? But let's take this somewhere private."

Mason, Lutalo and Mwamba followed Reth into the large hut from which he had first emerged. Inside the shelter there was a short, rectangular wooden table. Beaded ornaments, jewelry, carved and painted masks, and numerous bright feathers were scattered around an empty container, placed at the center of the table. Mason was fascinated by the beautiful crafts, especially the masks. Reth quickly swiped away the various objects to the floor, gently placed the wrapped- up bundle onto the table, and then carefully peeled away the cloth from the stone. The old man fell to his knees as he unveiled the package's contents.

Mwamba rushed toward his king. "Sir! Reth, are you all right!?"

Reth let out a slow, guttural, howl. Mason and Lutalo stepped back, unsure of what was happening to the kneeling king.

Reth remained silent for a few moments with his face buried in his arms, and then suddenly lifted his hands to the ceiling and shouted, "A double feast tonight!" With tears flowing like rivers through the canals of wrinkles on his face. "My friends, you have found it! A double feast! A double feast!" He began quickly pacing around the room. "For many years I have wondered and hoped that Akili was still alive, but I could never be certain. Villagers would sometimes bring me items from the jungle that they said proved he was still out there — up in his tree house — but still I could not tell if these items were genuine."

Mason and Lutalo looked at each other, both a little puzzled but excited too.

"Akili is an old friend of mine," the king continued. "Many years ago, a thief came and took this statue from my father's hut when he was the village leader. At the time, Akili and I were mere children, but we both decided to go and search for it. The statue had no special qualities or powers, but to us it was an important matter of justice that we recover what had been stolen from my father. We decided that the thief must have run off into the jungle — and we secretly left the next day. On our quest, though, we were separated. I decided to return to the village, but Akili never came back. I had never known what had happened to him or if he ever found the statue."

"Sir," Mason interrupted. "Akili, he, well, he was much older than you. Are you sure he is the same friend?"

Reth smiled at the boys. "I am pleased with the two of you, very pleased indeed. Thank you for returning the stone back to me. If you will please excuse me, boys, I am a little overwhelmed by the events of the day thus far. I will see you all in a few hours at our feast tonight — no, our double feast. Mwamba, could you please stay with me for a little while? I would like to talk to you a bit."

"Of course, sir," said Mwamba.

Lutalo grabbed Mason by the wrist. "Come on, I want you to meet my mother!" He rushed his friend out of the Reth's chambers and toward the hut where he had met Mason. As the three of them neared Lutalo's home, Mason could see a woman rocking in the same twisted throne of reeds and branches he had first seen Lutalo in. She had a blank stare on her face, but still her sad expression didn't take away from her beauty. "Wow!" Thought Mason. "She's pretty."

Lutalo let go of Mason and speeded up to a full sprint toward the woman. "Mama! Mama! I am home! We found the Zebra of Life!"

The woman turned toward Lutalo, keeping the same blank stare on her face. When he reached her, he threw his arms around her neck, and kissed her on the cheek. She slowly placed her hands on him, as if to check if he was real. She soon tightened her grip on the boy and began to cry and kiss the top of his head. "My son!" She whispered.

"Mama, this is my friend Mason," said Lutalo, pulling back from his mother's bear hug. "He is my cyber friend I told you about — from America. The one I knew I had to send a message to. He came, just like I knew he would, and has helped me, or actually I helped him rescue Father and the zebra. Father is at Reth's hut now. They are throwing a big celebration in our honor tonight. Oh, I forgot to tell you, Mason, my mother's name is Lewa."

"Slow down, son," his mother laughed. "It is an honor to meet you, Mason." And she extended her hand to him.

"The honor is all mine," said Mason.

"Well now! There's going to be a feast, eh? In honor of my boy and his friend. My goodness what a happy day this is."

"A double feast, Mama."

"Yes," she chuckled, "then you two had better go and wash up for this celebration."

"Come on, Mason. I'll show you where we can get cleaned up." Lutalo walked Mason around the back of his hut to a large wash bin. They splashed their faces clean and washed their necks and under their arms.

"Whew! I had no idea how dirty I was," said Mason, sniffing at his armpit. "Oh! And stinky."

After they had finished washing up, the boys and Lewa walked toward the center of the village. Sounds of music and song were already filling the air.

"It sounds like the party's already starting," said Mason. Suddenly he stopped walking. "You know, Lutalo, I've been meaning to tell you that I need to go home soon. I'm not sure how, but I would like it to be tonight. I miss my own mom." He pulled his red satchel off of his back, still filled with the golden bow and arrows, and handed it to Lutalo. "I want you to have these."

"Oh, no, Mason. I can't take them. You deserve to keep them."

"My brother Jamie wanted you to have them, and I promised him I'd give them to you. I want you to have them."

Lutalo slowly took the gift from his friend.

"What do you say, son?" Asked his mother.

"Thank you, Mason, and thank Jamie for me too, but if I get to keep these, then I want you to take something back with you too." Lutalo took one of the bamboo canteens out of the satchel and handed it to Mason. "Wait a minute; I want to give you one more thing." Lutalo ran back to his hut, leaving Mason alone with Lewa.

"I cannot tell you how grateful I am to you, Mason," she said. "You saved my husband, kept my boy safe, and restored the Zebra of Life to the village. You are a remarkable young man, and I'm so glad that my son has a friend like you." She wiped a few tears from her eyes as she continued to speak. "You will promise to keep writing won't you?"

Mason felt a little embarrassed, but smiled at the woman. "I promise."

Lutalo came running up to them, with one arm behind his back.

"What are you hiding?" Asked Mason.

"This." Lutalo handed Mason a brightly painted, beaded, and bejeweled mask. "I saw you looking at the things on Reth's table, and I could tell you really liked the masks. So I want you to have one." It was even more beautiful than any of the ones Mason had seen in Reth's hut.

"This is too cool," said Mason, running his hand over the many beads and jewels set in swirling designs around the eye holes of the mask.

"Boys! My little heroes! Come here; I want to show you something." Reth was leaning out of his hut just a few yards away from the threesome. He wildly waved them over to him.

As they entered the hut again, Mason and Lutalo immediately noticed Akili's walking stick leaning up against the back wall.

"Lutalo!" Mason gasped.

"I know! It's Akili's."

"But where is he?"

"Ahem," said a voice behind the boys. They turned to see who it was, but saw no one.

"Who's there?" Asked Mason.

"Over here, boys," said the voice.

"Where?" Asked Lutalo.

"Over here, by my cane."

They looked again toward the white walking stick.

"No, it can't be. Akili, is that you?" asked Lutalo.

The man nodded.

"But it can't be you. You look different. Younger, like Reth," said Mason.

"It is me," Akili answered. "I know I look different. It's from being in the tree house. Each day that I stayed up there, I aged faster and faster — faster than any normal human — but I couldn't leave. I could never leave until the stone statue was restored to its rightful owner. You see, the thief who stole the statue was a witch doctor, who put a curse on the statue. After Reth and I were separated on our quest for it, I was able to find that thief, and I tried to take the statue from him. But he used a spell to stop me, and he put me up in that tree house where I stayed. He told me that I would be able to leave once the statue was given back to its owner. It was all part of a game he was playing — an evil, senseless game."

"I'm glad you are free," said Mason, and Lutalo agreed.

Reth, Mwamba, and Lewa stepped up next to the boys. The king placed a hand on each of the boys' shoulders and squeezed them tightly. "Young men, I can't tell you how much I appreciate your bravery and willpower to succeed."

"We had a lot of help too," said Mason. "This has definitely been an adventure of a lifetime."

"I think it's time you both joined in the celebration. It's in your honor after all," said the old king.

Mason smiled at Reth and Akili, and gave a short bow to them.

"I'll be out in a minute, Mason," Lutalo called, as his friend exited the hut. He turned back to Akili and Reth. "Mason told me that he would like to go home tonight. Is there any way we can help him?"

"There is," answered Akili. "Take him to the shade tree at the front of the village when he says he is ready to leave."

Lutalo, his mother, father, king and old friend Akili went out of the tent and found Mason dancing with several villagers around a huge bonfire. Lutalo rushed up to him and said "Let's eat!"

After feasting on the freshly harvested crops that had been revived by the zebra's powers, Mason at last declared that he was ready to go home. "I will miss you and your people so much, Lutalo. But I miss my mom, my friends and even Jamie."

"I understand." Lutalo led Mason away from the party and stopped under the shade tree at the front of the village. "Akili told me to take you here when you were ready to go home. Do you have your canteen and the mask?"

"Yes … I'm really going to miss you."

"Me too."

"Tell everyone that I said goodbye, and that I'll never forget them. I promise to chat with you on Cyber Writers soon."

Lutalo sighed. "This is harder than when Jelani left us that first time."

"Yeah, but he did come back. We saw each other again." The two friends hugged each other warmly. "Until we meet again, my friend," said Mason.

Lutalo nodded. "Until we meet again."

Mason watched as his friend slowly walked back toward the party, until all he could see was the bright flame of the bonfire.

Mason was startled by a loud knocking on his door.

"Mason, it's time to get up!" said his mother. " I am not an alarm clock."

Mason pulled the covers down and grinned broadly. "What a great dream," he thought, until he rolled over and saw his bamboo canteen and beautiful African mask lying on his nightstand.

About the Author

Karen Kostlivy graduated from the University California Davis with a degree in Rhetoric and Communication. She enjoys spending time her family and listening to her two sons Camron and Masson play guitar. After a successful career in the private and public sector, Karen decided to return to a former passion, writing and creating stories for readers of all ages. She happily resides in Yuba City California with her husband Davis and youngest son.

Continue the Adventure at Your Local Library...